Lost Magic

The Natural Order: Book 3

R.J. Vickers

Cover art by Amber Elizabeth Lamoureaux
Cover design by Maduranga

www.RJVickers.com
For orders, please email: **r.j.vickers@comcast.net**

ISBN: 1539958426
ISBN-13: 978-1539958420

Chapter 1

Escape

While the rest of the students were upstairs for dinner, Tristan and Amber made for the Subroom, silent and jittery. Drakewell expected them back in the Map Room in thirty minutes. They had that much time to pack their belongings and prepare for the arduous journey through the mountains.

They were not allowed to say goodbye. They had to vanish without a trace.

"Something is going to go wrong," Tristan muttered as he pulled his fraying backpack open. "I don't think we're ever going to see the Lair again."

"You don't know that," Amber said quietly, eyes downcast.

Trying to set aside his misgivings, Tristan began throwing as many warm layers as he could fit into his backpack. It was still early spring, so they would be walking through snow as they crossed the high pass to Millersville. The last they had seen, Millersville had been a smoldering ruin. Tristan hoped some fragment of the village had survived.

Once he had crammed all of his clothes into the threadbare pack, along with his compass and water bottle, Tristan bent to lace up his hiking boots. Before long, he and Amber would be trying to persuade Drakewell's nemesis that they wanted to join her. He couldn't see how it would work—Ilana was far too cunning to be taken in by whatever lie they came up with. But this was their only hope.

Shaking away these grim thoughts, Tristan fetched a handful of marbles from the vase in the back of the room. "How many do you think we'll need?" he asked Amber.

"As few as possible," she said. "We shouldn't give the magicians any advantage."

Grabbing another fistful just out of habit, Tristan turned to give the Subroom a final look. He had a feeling he would never see it like this again. There were the mattresses crammed haphazardly along the far wall, piled with pillows and quilts; there was the bookshelf, with its carefully scavenged collection; there was the table Tristan had fixed in his first year; and there, in the corner, lay his schoolbag with its unfinished homework and battered textbooks. He would give anything to return to the innocence of last year, when his main troubles had been working through homework and avoiding punishment.

"The others will return from dinner soon," Amber whispered.

Reluctantly, Tristan slung his backpack over one shoulder and followed Amber through the Prasidimum barrier, leaving their brightly-lit home behind. He half-hoped Leila might return from dinner early, wondering where he had gone, and he would get a chance to give her one last hug goodbye.

Just as they reached the main corridor and turned down the stairs towards Delair's mine and the Map Room, Tristan heard the clamor of his friends returning from dinner. He quickened his pace, glancing over his shoulder to be sure they had not been seen. At last they escaped into the depths of Delair's mine, shrouded by the chill darkness.

Drakewell was waiting for them in the Map Room, a bundle of food at his feet.

"This should last you a week," he said, spilling the contents onto the floor. "If you have not reached your destination by then, you would be wise to hurry. These mountains are unforgiving in spring. Despite our best efforts, you could run across avalanches and flooding streams as the snow begins to melt."

Tristan and Amber dropped to their knees and began shoving energy bars, peanut butter, and tortillas into their already-bulging packs.

"Ashton, are you capable of boiling water without a stove?" Drakewell asked.

Amber blinked at him. "I suppose. I've never tried."

"Very well." He added a pack of dried pasta to the stack, along with a bag of lentils and another of rice.

"Guard that phone number with your life," Drakewell told Tristan. "It is our only hope."

Tristan reached a hand into his pocket to ensure the

crumpled slip of paper Ilana had given him was still there.

Crossing to the nearest stone table, which had taken the shape of a craggy ring of mountains, Drakewell indicated the town of Millersville near the far left-hand corner. "You can set an Intralocation spell to track the town, but do not take the quickest route. At this time of year, the high mountains are safer than the lower hills, since the snow will still be solidly frozen. If you try to head downhill instead of up, you will have to cross two wide rivers that may have already shed their ice." He handed them each a pair of crampons, which Tristan tied to the outside of his pack. "That pass is the most straightforward. You could walk over it with no difficulty in summer, and you should not encounter any problems now. Try to make it to the top before sunrise tomorrow. If you remain too close to the school, we would be accused of letting you go too easily."

Natasha slipped into the Map Room just then, bolting the door behind her. "Leila has been asking after you, Tristan," she said. "I informed her that you're working off a few hours of punishment with Gracewright, but that you should be back by midnight. Best start moving now, before anyone gets suspicious."

To Tristan's surprise, she drew him and Amber into a brief embrace. "Good luck. You'll need it."

Leaving the two professors behind, Tristan and Amber started up the stairs towards the ballroom. Tristan expected at every turn to be accosted by a teacher who demanded explanations, but the halls were empty. Even the ballroom was dim and silent, the tables wiped clean for the night.

Up in the meadow, the first stars were beginning to emerge, dulled by a near-full moon. Though the snow had melted from the meadow, the mountains were still cloaked with an icy sheen that glowed in the moonlight.

"It's that pass, right?" Tristan asked, pointing to a low ridge that lay west of the school.

Amber nodded.

"Let's worry about the Intralocation spell later. For now we can just head that way."

Pulling on his wool hat, which Gracewright had knitted for him the previous winter, Tristan led the way forward along the damp forest floor. The ground was strewn with rotting pine needles, the trees still hiding the odd patch of snow. Though the trees stifled some of the wind, it was still bitingly cold, and before long Tristan had dug out his gloves and scarf. Amber did not seem to mind the cold; the wind riffled through her white hair and turned her cheeks red, but she did not fetch her own hat.

"They'll never believe us," Tristan said as they trudged past endless rows of pines. "We got away too easily. And why would we leave, after all this time?"

"Maybe we were tortured," Amber said. "If we were punished for using the Map Room without permission, and tied up in the tunnels, it would make sense that we escaped."

"They won't believe that," Tristan said. "Unless we have marks." He gave Amber a sideways look. "Is that what you're suggesting?"

She chewed on her lip. "Well, if we had lines around our wrists where we had been tied up, that would be enough."

Tristan made a face. "I suppose it won't matter if we do anything now. I can't feel my legs to begin with."

"Tomorrow," Amber said quietly. "Once we have left the valley."

Up they climbed, across the gradually sloping valley, while around them the trees began to shrink and thin out and beneath them the snow rose to overtake the bare ground. At last they reached the base of the ridge, where the last of the trees ended and a blank expanse of snow beckoned. Tristan sat on a snow-covered rock and strapped on his crampons, Amber copying him after a moment's pause. They would have to be careful—if they slipped and slashed their legs open with the cruel claws of the crampons, there would be no one to help them. Even Amber's magic might be unequal to replacing lost blood.

Slowly, eyeing the top of the ridge, Tristan started to climb. He felt as though they had already walked all night, yet the sky showed no sign of lightening. Before long he was sweating from exertion, and he peeled off first his hat and then his gloves and scarf. He wished for ski poles, branches, anything to help keep his balance, but it was too late to search for walking sticks. The forest was far behind.

As they climbed, a dark wave of clouds billowed from the western sky and slowly engulfed the stars.

"I bet that's Drakewell," Tristan panted, stopping to catch his. "If he's smart, he'll send a snowstorm to cover our tracks."

Amber nodded, breathing hard.

"I hope he gives us a bit longer before it starts snowing. It'll be miserable if we're stuck up here in a blizzard." Tristan kneaded the knot in his side with his fist.

Before long, the clouds bubbled to the eastern horizon, cloaking the moon in shadow and extinguishing every glimpse of light. Amber did not seem to mind, but when Tristan tried to fumble his way blindly forward, he tripped and fell face-forward into the snow.

"Sorry," Amber said, the crunch of her footsteps pausing. A second later, the air around her began glowing with a soft radiance, as though she had magnified her aura a hundred times over. Still half-blind, Tristan stumbled to his feet and followed the strange light.

At last they reached the ridge, which had a steeper drop down the opposite side. As they began to pick their way down, the sky lightened. Now that they had made their way safely out of the valley, a wave of exhaustion hit Tristan; he would happily have lain down on the exposed slope to sleep.

Just as he thought this, the first gentle snowflake landed and melted on his icy cheek. Tristan pulled on his hat and gloves once more, the sweat from their climb quickly cooling.

Finally, with the sky growing almost imperceptibly lighter behind the clouds, Tristan and Amber reached the base of the ridge. Here the trees were taller and more densely packed, and they were immediately protected from the wind.

Drakewell hadn't given them a tent—Tristan supposed that would have looked too suspicious—so they crawled into the sheltered space beneath a pine's wide boughs.

Without eating anything, Amber lay down on the bed of dried pine needles, hugging her knees. Tristan settled down behind her, his knees pressed into the backs of hers for warmth, and as the night grew later he moved closer until his chest was resting against her spine. He could feel her breathing beneath the layers of her coat, and every inch of his skin tingled with the warmth of her body beside his. A braver version of him would have slipped an arm around her waist and nestled his chin against her cheek, but he was paralyzed. Amber was just barely shorter than he was, and their bodies fit together like puzzle pieces. Every moment he imagined she might shy away, but when she shifted in her sleep, she simply nestled in closer.

Beyond the shelter of the pine boughs, the wind began to howl.

Tristan woke to a blinding shaft of sunlight. The snow-storm had ended, and their tree-cave was buried deeper than before under a new drift. Amber was still asleep, so Tristan shifted gently, trying not to disturb her. He gulped down half a bottle of water and refilled it with snow, flexing his fingers to see if they retained any feeling.

"Morning," Amber murmured from behind him, stirring beneath her layers.

"I didn't mean to wake you," Tristan said, settling back

against his pack.

Rubbing her eyes, Amber sat up. "We should get going now anyway. I don't want to walk all night again."

"Me neither," Tristan said. "Want some oatmeal?"

With hardly a thought, Amber set the icy water boiling and cooked their oatmeal into a sad, lumpy mush. Drakewell had not given them anything to put with the oatmeal, but at least it was hot and filling.

Tristan was still thinking about the way he had slept curled against Amber, sharing her warmth. Although Amber acted as though nothing had happened, a smile played at her lips as she packed away the dried oats.

Once they had stowed their supplies and strapped the crampons to their packs, Tristan set an Intralocation spell to track the town of Millersville. He focused on the Aspen Lodge, where they had stayed for several weeks the past year, imagining its brightly-lit dining room and stone fireplace. Of course, it was likely reduced to rubble now. They could be heading to a ghost town.

"You ready?" he asked Amber, releasing the marble to hover before him and hooking his thumbs beneath his straps.

"Ready enough," she said. "I—I wish we could just vanish into these woods. Drakewell would never know. We could escape and forget about all of this."

Tristan's heart leapt. She had as good as admitted she would be happy just running away and spending the rest of her days with him. "Until Ilana destroys everything," he said grimly, trying not to think of what could be. "We're part of this mess. We can't just ignore it."

"I know," Amber said. "It was just a useless wish."

Tristan gave her a sad smile. "I'd love nothing more."

His legs aching from the previous day's climb, Tristan set out across the crisp new layer of snow. While Amber trod her usual path on the surface of the snow, leaving no sign of her passage, Tristan plodded along through the drifts, occasionally plunging waist-deep through the icy crust hidden beneath the new snow.

They stopped briefly for a cold lunch of tortillas and peanut butter, and Tristan was reluctant to re-shoulder his pack afterwards. His knees had taken a beating from the long downhill slog yesterday and protested with every step through the brittle snow. He was grateful when the sun began setting behind the mountains ahead. With the purple haze of sunset fading around them, they sought out another dry patch beneath the boughs of a pine and began to prepare a dinner of unseasoned rice. Tristan's stomach was grumbling hollowly; he missed Quinsley and Leila's cooking.

As the rice boiled away, Tristan dug in his pack for the length of rope Drakewell had given them.

"Time to give ourselves rope burn," he said with a grimace. If this was to look convincing, the rope marks would have to appear several days old by the time they reached Millersville. "We were tied up for a week before we got out, okay?"

Amber nodded slowly.

"And we were tied to the ceiling, so we couldn't sleep

that whole time. Drakewell's gone completely mad—we couldn't wait to get out."

"They'll question us," Amber said. "Torture us, most likely. Were we locked in the same room?"

"Sure," Tristan said. "That's how we got out—you finally drew on your own magic to break us free. But it knocked you out, so I had to carry you out of the Lair. I don't want them knowing how strong you are."

"I can hardly use my powers underground as it is," Amber said. "I have to draw on the life around me. In the Lair, I could only draw on myself and the other students."

"It'll be more believable, then," Tristan said.

Amber hugged her arms unhappily across her chest. "It also means I'll be helpless if we're taken underground again. We will be entirely at Ilana's mercy."

Tristan shivered at the thought. Picking at the end of the rope, he said, "Do you want to tie me up to that tree? If I spend the night tied up, it'll look more believable."

With a grimace, Amber knelt behind Tristan and knotted the rope tightly about his wrists. His skin tingled each time her hands brushed against his. When he stood, she looped the rope over a branch and secured it in place.

Tristan stood like that, arms stretched painfully behind him, for all of fifteen minutes. Then he said, "Forget it. This is miserable. Can you untie me?"

"A week," Amber said, her lips twitching. "We would both be dead by then."

Once he was untied from the tree, Tristan wriggled one hand out of its binding. Grabbing the knot on the other, he gave the rope a sharp tug.

He cursed as the rope bit into his flesh. He gave it another tug, yanking the rope around his wrist so it sliced deeper than before. The fibers were sharp and splintery, and he was sure several of them had embedded themselves under his skin.

Breathing hard, he undid the knot and let the rope fall to his side. Just as he hoped, the rope had left a raw line where it had cut into him. With any luck, that would still show by the time they reached Millersville.

The second wrist was even more painful than the first, since he knew exactly what to expect. Biting his tongue, Tristan tried unsuccessfully to stifle his yell of pain.

When Amber's turn came, she screwed her eyes shut and gave the rope a fierce tug. She let out a quiet gasp of pain but did not complain.

"You're braver than me," Tristan said wryly. "If they don't believe us…"

They settled in to eat their charred rice in silence. Tristan kept flinching as his sleeves rasped against his raw skin, but any efforts to bandage or heal the open wounds would render their efforts useless.

"They might not let us talk to each other once they've found us," Tristan said at last. "It might be lonely as hell. They'll be watching us every second."

Amber nodded, her eyes wide and pensive. "What day are we allowed to attack the Lair?"

"The tenth of every month," Tristan said flatly. He wasn't about to forget that soon. That was the day when he would convince his friends once and for all that he had turned against them. Only he and Amber knew how to shatter the protective barriers around the Lair; only he and Amber could do any genuine damage from afar. Alldusk's worst fears would be confirmed. And Leila would never forgive him.

After that, their days fell into a rhythm. For six days they trudged through periods of sun interspersed with snow flurries, their packs growing steadily lighter as they depleted their rations. Tristan had no idea when they would reach the supply town, but he hoped it would be soon. They would not last much longer.

They spent every night curled together beneath a tree or under a protective shelf of rock, each day plodding through the endless forest. Tristan's marbles were nearing the end of their supply as well; he went through two a day, and before long they would be reduced to following the sun.

The weight of their task had settled over Tristan, and he was too miserable to spare the energy for conversation, as much as he treasured his time with Amber. They spoke very little, only "Good morning" and "Still have all your toes?" when they woke, and "Does this look like a good campsite?" and "Goodnight" when they stopped each day. His thoughts were fixed on the day they would be fetched by Ilana's followers. Everything would end then, and it seemed useless to pretend otherwise.

"I'm glad you're here with me," Amber said one night

as they were washing out their cooking pot with snow.

"I'm glad you're here, too," Tristan said, leaning towards her so their elbows brushed together. "And not just because you can use your magic to keep us safe if anything happens."

Amber smiled shyly. "I think we'll reach the village tomorrow. I don't know why I know that."

"Damn it. I wish we *could* just run away." His stomach twisted every time he thought of what awaited them in Millersville.

"You know we could," Amber breathed.

Tristan shook his head. Ever since Amber had suggested it, the thought had tormented him. It would be so easy to turn south and find another town to shelter in. They could find Tristan's mother and figure out what to do from there. If they had to, they could even move up to the Alaskan wilderness to escape their own criminal records. They were more than familiar enough with mountains and snow to manage that.

But he could never live with himself if he abandoned the Lair. In the back of his mind, he would always be counting down the days until the world ended. At the rate Ilana's magicians were working, it would not take much longer.

This had become his life—this single-minded, insane mission—and he would rather die than see it fall to pieces. He had not become heartless through his work at the Lair, as he had feared; instead, he was beginning to care too much.

"If it was just you, by yourself, would you have run off?" Tristan asked.

Amber hung her head. "I think so. You're a better person than me, Tristan. I'm afraid. I've always been so afraid."

Tristan set aside the slush-filled pot and put an arm around Amber's waist. He half expected her to shy away—instead she leaned into him, head on his shoulder, and stared up at the darkening sky.

"I'm sorry to be dragging you into this," he said softly. "But I think you're incredibly brave to do it."

Amber leaned in closer still, her silvery hair cold against Tristan's neck. He wanted to put his arms around her and kiss her and forget everything else, but tonight was not the time.

They sat like that for a long time, while the stars winked to life overhead and the slush in their pot hardened to sludgy ice. With the moon still hidden behind a ragged line of mountains, the Milky Way dominated the night sky, a swath of hazy brilliance strewn with billions of stars.

When a shooting star painted a fleeting line across the sky, Amber lifted her head and turned to look at Tristan. He kissed her on the forehead, her skin soft and smooth. A thrill ran through him, an icy jolt that had nothing to do with the temperature.

Amber breathed in a gasp of surprise.

"For luck," he said.

He might have imagined it, but her eyes seemed to glisten with tears.

"Goodnight, Amber."

Chapter 2

Ilana's Stronghold

They reached Millersville far too soon. It was hardly midmorning when the first clue of the town's proximity revealed itself—a whiff of ashes stirred up in the brisk wind. As they picked their way closer, Tristan held his breath, hoping the place was not deserted.

The first thing he saw was the Aspen Lodge, nothing more than a charred frame half-crumbled to the ground. Farther on, though, he saw trails of smoke rising from chimneys. The village lived on.

They picked up their pace as they drew closer still, eager for news and warmth and food. Among the rations, Tristan had discovered a pile of gold dollars, enough to buy them a hearty meal before they were fetched by Ilana.

At the town's only café, the owner greeted Tristan and Amber with some confusion.

"Weren't you here with that school group a month ago?"

"Yeah," Tristan said. "And we've gotten lost. We have

to call someone to come pick us up."

"Phone's over there," he said dubiously. "Did you make it out okay after the fire?"

Tristan nodded. "You guys too?"

"More or less. We've had a few people airlifted for treatment, but no deaths."

Tristan was relieved to hear that. Though it had not been his professors who set the fire, it was their school's fault for dragging Millersville into this mess.

Setting his backpack on a barstool, he dug for the pouch of dollar coins Drakewell had slipped him. "Can we get something to eat? We're starving."

When Tristan dumped the entire contents of the purse on the table—some thirty dollars in all—the owner cleared his throat and vanished into the kitchen.

Tristan turned to Amber. "I guess I should call Ilana now. She'll take a while to get here. If she's still planning to take us, that is."

Amber's eyes widened. "So soon?"

When he met her eyes, he could still feel the cold touch of her skin on his lips. He wished he had been brave enough to give her a real kiss. Swallowing, he tore his gaze from hers and turned to the phone sitting on its stand. They probably didn't have cell phone service in a town this remote. With trembling hands, he pulled the phone number from his pocket and dialed.

The phone rang eight times, long enough that Tristan was about to give up.

Then, suddenly, the sound stopped. "Hello?" said a

thickly-accented male voice.

Tristan gulped. "I—um—do you know Ilana?"

"Yes," the man said with more enthusiasm than before.

"Well, she told us to call if we ever—if we changed our minds."

"Yes?"

"We've run away." Tristan glanced at Amber, whose unblinking gaze was fixed on him. "We want to join Ilana."

"I see!" The man's voice was triumphant. "Where should I collect you?"

"In Millersville," Tristan said. "That town you burned down."

"Right. And you're sure you're not going to back out of this?"

"No," Tristan said, with more confidence than he felt. "We're never going back there again."

"Brilliant! See you in a couple hours. Stay where you are, 'k?"

"Okay."

The man hung up, leaving Tristan frozen in place with the phone still held to his ear. He had done it. There was no going back now.

"How long?" Amber asked quietly.

"Two hours." Slowly he lowered the phone back into its stand and returned to the bar, where he sank onto a stool and rested his chin on his hands.

They were just finishing a second round of coffees when the door jingled and opened to admit a sandy-haired young man with a beard and the rough face of a miner. Until he turned straight towards Tristan and Amber, who were sitting in a corner booth, Tristan had assumed he was a local.

"You're the one who called," the man said. "Anton." He held out his hand, which Tristan shook, getting to his feet. "And you are?"

"Tristan," he said. "And this is Amber."

The man's eyes gleamed. "Of course you are." Now that Tristan could hear him in person, he thought the man sounded Irish. "Ilana said you'd come, but I didn't believe her. She's returned to our base, of course. Didn't have any time to lose. And you're really hoping to join us?"

"Yes," Tristan said firmly.

"Very well, then. Let's get going. Unless you wanted to finish your coffees, that is."

Tristan pushed his mug away. "I've had enough of that to last me two weeks." He tried to feign friendliness, afraid that his voice would crack at any moment and give away his fear.

With a chuckle, Anton turned and led the way from the café. They walked past sleepy houses—some still showing scars from the firebomb attack—and through a grove of aspens on the way to the familiar airstrip. A tiny airplane stood waiting, emblazoned with some sort of company name in what might have been Icelandic.

"It's going to be a long flight, I'll warn you," Anton said, patting the wing of his plane. "I've picked up a bit of food to tide you over, but it won't be much fun anyway."

He didn't seem too concerned about this.

Tristan followed Amber up the ladder into the body of the nine-seater plane. He had never flown in a plane this small before, but judging from the flimsy-looking frame, he suspected the journey would be bumpy.

"It's going to be loud," Anton said, jumping into the pilot's seat. "You can wear the headphones on your seat. That way I can talk to you, too."

Settling his backpack onto the seat in front of him, Tristan sat and clamped the heavy headset over his ears. His pair had a small microphone as well, which he folded out of the way.

"All settled?" Anton asked, his voice buzzing through the headphones. "Comfortable enough?"

Tristan gave him a thumbs-up, while Amber curled her legs beside her on the seat.

As Tristan had expected, the plane was flung from side to side as it climbed into the air. They made it past a low-lying band of clouds, but never broke through the higher clouds. Instead, Anton set a course not too far above the ground—just about level with the mountain peaks they were heading towards—which provided them with plenty of turbulence to jolt the plane at annoyingly regular intervals.

Once they had more or less leveled out, Anton turned and said, "You getting on all right?"

Tristan nodded.

"Why did you run off, then? Change of heart?"

Tristan grimaced and lowered his microphone again.

"Drakewell's hated me ever since I first got there. I don't know why. He told me and Amber to stay in the Map Room and watch what happened during the fight, and he said we were absolutely not allowed to use the globe. But we flooded the cave."

"That was *you?*" Anton sounded intrigued. "Blimey, you're a talented pair."

Tristan's face went hot. "Well, Drakewell didn't think so. He was furious. He locked us up in the tunnels and tied us to the ceiling. It was miserable." He drew back one of his sleeves to show the rope burn. "We just escaped a week ago, and we've been trying to get somewhere to call you guys ever since."

"Ooh," Anton said, clicking his tongue. "That looks bloody painful. How'd you get out?"

Tristan readjusted the microphone, letting his sleeve fall back into place. "Amber used her own magic to cut through the ropes. She passed out, so I had to carry her all the way out of the Lair and into the woods. She woke up once we were outside, so we went and grabbed a few things from a store-room and sneaked out. I don't think Drakewell started looking for us until the next afternoon, so we made it out of the valley before he figured out we were gone."

"And he didn't come after you?"

"I don't know," Tristan said. "He might've tried. If we'd stayed in that town any longer, they probably would've found us."

"Lucky buggers, you are."

"Yeah," Tristan said. "Thank god we made it out of there. When Amber passed out, I thought—" He trailed off for dramatic effect, glancing at Amber.

She met his eyes with a cornered look. What was she afraid of? Tristan thought he was doing a very good job with this whole charade. Besides, Anton seemed a lot nicer than Tristan had expected.

They didn't speak much more after that. Two hours into the flight, they landed to refuel, and again two hours after that. The sun was behind them, and they hadn't passed over an ocean yet, so Tristan figured they were heading east towards New York. Again and again they landed to refuel, until night fell and Tristan began to doze, his neck cricked at an uncomfortable angle. He lost track of how many stops they made, but at one point he thought he saw the ocean gleaming in the moonlight far below.

It was still night when they landed, and it took Tristan a moment to realize they had reached their final destination, not merely another refueling location. He climbed stiffly down the ladder, trying to figure out where they were in the dim light cast from the lights at the end of the plane's wings. If he wasn't mistaken, he thought they stood on a flat expanse of ice with the faint outline of ridges in the distance. Somewhere far north, then. Ilana must have thought of the Lair when she chose the location of her own base.

"You must be exhausted," Anton said. "Ilana knows you're arriving. She should be here to greet you in a moment."

Sure enough, a spot of light appeared ahead of them on the ice and quickly grew larger as it approached.

"Tristan and Amber. Welcome."

Tristan recognized the voice before he could make out Ilana's face. This time her tone was soft, almost gentle. Had he been mistaken about her?

"I would love to talk to you both," she continued, "but first you should sleep. You've had a very long flight."

Tristan barely restrained himself from asking where they were. That would immediately have raised suspicion. Instead he said, "Thank you."

"Good job, darling," Ilana told Anton, kissing him lightly on the cheek. "I'll see you tomorrow."

Tristan and Amber followed Ilana across the ice—he was sure now that it was ice, because it crunched underfoot—until they reached a round trapdoor that seemed to be carved from the ice itself. Down a ladder, they entered a round tunnel through the ice that made Tristan feel like a rabbit in its warren. Oddly enough, the air that wafted through the ice-cave was warm. From there, he lost track of the twisting, mazelike route they took through the warren, which ended up at a pair of comfortable rooms, the beds heaped with quilts and blankets.

"Sleep well," Ilana said. "I'll fetch you in the morning."

She left Tristan and Amber standing outside their rooms, both a bit dazed.

"Do you think she's just tricking us?" Tristan whispered. "Or was Drakewell wrong?"

"I think it's a trick," Amber said. "But we might as well

play along."

Making a face, Tristan turned to his room. "Goodnight."

He lay awake late into the night, puzzling over what was happening. This was not what he had expected at all. Anton had been so kind to them, and he hadn't even questioned their story. Now Ilana was nothing but generous and welcoming. Had they been wrong?

Nonetheless, Tristan got a very strange feeling from this ice-cave. He and Amber would have to tread carefully.

Chapter 3

The Harvest

When Tristan woke the next morning and ventured from his room, still wearing the same filthy clothes he had worn since leaving the Lair, he found a small girl waiting for him in the hallway. She was much younger than any of Tristan's classmates, no more than ten, and she had the fair complexion and pale blue eyes of a Scandinavian.

"Breakfast is ready," she said in a commanding tone that belied her small stature. "Is your friend awake?"

"I'll check." He rapped softly on Amber's door, which opened a moment later. Her hair was tousled and her eyes bleary; she had clearly just woken. Combing a finger through her hair, she joined them in the hallway. Tristan tried not to meet her eyes, wary of revealing how much he cared for her. It was a weapon Ilana could easily use against him.

"Are there any other clothes we could change into?" he asked quickly. "I don't want to bother you, but we're a bit smelly."

The girl blinked at him. "Yes." She took them down two corridors and through three doorways to a side room, where a hundred or so uniforms were piled on shelves. Each uniform was in the same style as the girl's clothes— tan pants and a white long-sleeved shirt, sorted by size. Tristan found a pair that looked as though it fit and changed behind a shelf. The girl indicated a set of heavy fur boots by the wall, which Tristan gladly slipped on, leaving his battered hiking boots behind.

When Amber emerged from behind the second row of shelves, Tristan gave her a fleeting smile. She looked very pretty in the new uniform. They each grabbed a tan coat from a hook on their way out—Tristan had been expecting a heavy parka, but the soft deerskin jacket was light and thin.

"How long have you been here?" Tristan asked the girl as she led them back the way they'd come.

"I've always lived here," she said. "Ilana took me in when my parents died."

"That's generous of her," Tristan said dubiously. "Do you like it here?"

"Oh, yes."

From the finality of her tone, Tristan surmised that she did not wish to answer any more questions.

The dining room was a long chamber with a curving roof—it reminded Tristan of a miniature hangar. About twenty adults shared one table, while nearly fifty students of all ages filled the other five. Tristan swallowed. This was worse than Drakewell had feared.

No one paid them any heed, so Tristan scanned the room for empty seats. There were only two, on opposite sides of the room. Nervous and feeling entirely out-of-place, he slipped into one of the two empty seats between two older boys. Many of the students glanced his way, but none openly stared. As he helped himself to the food he could reach, he realized that no one was talking. Aside from the soft clank of forks against plates, the hall was silent. Tristan didn't know what to look at, so he stared at his plate, wondering what the others were thinking.

From what he had seen in his cursory look around the room, he had been surprised to find that Ilana's students represented what seemed like every race imaginable. Looking out of the corner of his eye, he tried to guess where the nearest students were from, though he couldn't be certain. He thought one kid looked Indian, and another could have been Korean. There were young kids, too, younger than could possibly have been dragged from any juvenile detention center. Ilana must be using a different method to recruit her students, then.

As he finished off his breakfast, Tristan glanced inadvertently across the room at Amber. She sat rigidly, like an ice sculpture, her fork lying untouched beside her plate. He would have given anything to know what she was thinking.

Just then, the students rose as one—breakfast was clearly over. Ilana beckoned Tristan and Amber to join her at the head table, where she gave them each a mug of hot chocolate that helped wash down the taste of oily eggs.

"I trust you slept well?"

"Yes, thank you," Tristan said, still trying to puzzle the woman out.

"Good. If you feel ready, I can assign you to work straight away."

Tristan glanced at Amber. "Okay."

She handed them each a printed schedule for the week. "My students are separated into five divisions based on talent. You will both join the first division. Each takes a turn at various tasks throughout the week, with lessons interspersed between these."

Looking down at his schedule, Tristan saw blocks of time labeled with activities such as "Harvesting" (the most common), "Kitchen duty," "Cleaning," "Strength training," and "Lessons." He wasn't sure if "harvesting" referred to food or magic.

"Your division is currently harvesting water magic," Ilana said, answering his question before he had a chance to ask. "If you follow me, I'll show you where. Every Wednesday and Friday evening, you two will join me for private lessons. I want to see what you're capable of." Her smile betrayed the slightest hint of a predatory gleam. "Do you have any questions?"

Tristan shook his head. It was best not to appear too curious.

They were led through the tunnels again; within two turns, Tristan had lost his way. Would they really be harvesting water magic? Drakewell would be amazed to learn the art wasn't lost after all.

Eventually Ilana stopped at a ladder, where they climbed out of the warren onto a vast, flat expanse of ice.

"Where are we?" Tristan asked. A second later he regretted the question.

Ilana smiled. "I don't mind telling you. We're in Greenland, in the far north. I've stabilized the ice around our cave so it doesn't melt. This is the last place in the world your professors would think to look for us."

That much was true. Who would be mad enough to build a stronghold in a quickly-eroding mass of ice?

Of course, if Ilana's magicians managed to wipe out humanity before the ice had fully melted, they could relocate to wherever suited them best. They could even move into the White House or Buckingham Palace if they wanted.

Now that he knew how many magicians Ilana had under her thumb, he didn't think they would find much in the way of opposition.

Ilana pointed to a huddle of shapes in the distance. From here they could have been seals or puffins. "There is the rest of the First Division. You can join them now, and I'll see you at lunch. Best of luck."

Tristan and Amber started in the direction of the class, looking straight ahead in case Ilana was watching them. Once they had gone some distance from the school, Tristan glanced over his shoulder and saw that they were alone.

"What do you think?" he asked softly.

"I think they're just waiting for us to make a mistake,"

Amber said. "We must tread very carefully."

Tristan nodded. "I don't think we'll get much time alone."

"No. That would encourage the students to think for themselves."

Tristan wanted to linger out on the ice, away from the watchful eye of Ilana's magicians, but they were close enough that the First Division would be able to see if they delayed. Reluctantly he continued on, straightening his spine and staring straight ahead as he had seen the other students do. So far, this was going much better than he had feared. If they kept quiet and stayed out of trouble, they might just pull this off.

"Welcome," a burly man called, waving to Tristan and Amber. He sounded German. "Will you be okay on your own?" he asked his division.

Six heads nodded.

Crossing over to Tristan and Amber, the man slapped Tristan on the shoulder. "Fresh blood! Our class is very small. We don't get enough talented students here. I am Stefan. And I already know all about you."

Tristan grimaced.

"What was that face? We are very excited to have you here!" He gestured to the students behind him. "There is so much you can teach us."

Tristan doubted that, though he knew they would go crazy if Amber ever let on how much she knew. "How are you collecting water magic, then?" he asked.

"Ah! So Ilana was correct! Your headmaster did not

rediscover that ancient art." Stefan leaned closer as though sharing a secret. "This is why we built our base here. Sometime in the past hundred thousand years, the ice sheet in Greenland has trapped a very large quantity of water magic. As the ice melts, it gives off vapor, which escapes from the nearest vent."

Glancing behind him, Tristan realized the students were clustered around a gap where a stream emerged from the iridescent blue ice. When he looked closer, he thought he could see a hazy blue mist rising from the opening.

"What happens when the ice sheet is gone?" he asked.

"Ah," Stefan said. "We figure that the only true use for magic is to keep humans in check. When the human population is no longer a threat, magic will no longer be needed. The earth's balance will not be destroyed."

"Haven't we already done that?" Tristan said. "It's not going to fix everything, is it? Getting rid of people, I mean."

"No. But the longer we wait, the longer the earth takes to recover."

In abstract terms, what Stefan said actually made sense. That was the disturbing part about it. There were probably quite a few environmentalists out there who would fully endorse Ilana's plans—provided, of course, that they were given a place in her new world.

"You can see the vapor, right?" Stefan asked.

"Yes," Tristan and Amber said together.

"Perfect. Our students can't pass above the Fourth Division until they learn to collect vapors. You may fetch a jar and begin harvesting."

Just then, Tristan noticed a wide sled piled with empty glass jars. "How old are the students when they start here?" he asked, thinking about the tiny girl who had led them to dinner.

"Oh, we start them as young as we can," Stefan said. "We have rescued many of them from orphanages. Ilana told us that, back at your Lair, some students with the potential for magic never developed any true abilities. But we found that when you begin before they can walk, the children have no time to develop any mental blocks to magic. Every single one of our students is able to confidently see auras and use magic within a few years."

It was a smart idea, Tristan had to admit. That way, the children would be so completely indoctrinated that they wouldn't have any objections to what they were doing. For all he knew, they weren't fully aware of life outside their rabbit-warren.

No one talked as they worked, but the six students shuffled politely aside to give Tristan and Amber space to access the mouth of the stream. They spent the next hour and a half filling jar after jar, chasing each wisp of vapor until they had filled the glass. It was tedious work, much less interesting than burning things in Alldusk's class, though it was fascinating to see the pale blue marbles form for the first time.

They remained out by the river until Tristan's extremities had gone numb and his face was stripped raw from the perpetual wind. Somehow, though they wore no more layers than he did, the other students didn't seem to mind.

On the tramp back to the ice cave, two of the students pulled the sled piled with jars while Stefan fell into step beside Tristan.

"The other students use a bit of their own magic to keep warm," Stefan said as Tristan blew on his hands in a desperate attempt to revive them. "This is a good little exercise to get them adept at using their internal strength without losing consciousness. After enough practice, they can perform large-scale spells with no trouble."

Tristan let his vision blur as he focused on drawing heat from within; after a moment, a bead of warmth blossomed in his hands. When he tried to send it through the rest of his body, his head began to spin. He stopped immediately.

Stefan led them down the ladder, where they abandoned the sled, and towards a room so deep in the ice that Tristan was surprised they didn't reach solid ground—or the ocean. This one was set up like a small gym, with weights and jump-ropes and pull-up bars.

"Another way to boost your internal magic reserves," Stefan said, taking a stance at the front of the room, "is with physical strength training. The stronger you are, the more energy you can safely burn through."

By this point, Tristan guessed that Stefan was permanently assigned to the First Division. He didn't mind—Stefan seemed reasonable enough. Normal, in fact. This was not at all what Tristan had expected from Ilana's school.

Thinking back to his arrival at the Lair, Tristan remembered being frightened by the magic and intimidated by Drakewell. It wasn't too hard to imagine that Drakewell had tricked them into choosing the wrong side.

Then again, the other professors supported Drakewell. Alldusk and Quinsley and Gracewright and Delair couldn't all be wrong. Could they?

Tristan and Amber took their places at the back of the gym, where they would be able to watch the other students, and proceeded to run through a brutal exercise regimen. The training lasted a full two hours, with brief water breaks every twenty minutes, and Tristan was ready to fall over by the end of the first hour. To his chagrin, the other students seemed unfazed by the endless rounds of weight-lifting and sprints and jumping jacks and push-ups. Even the skinny boy who looked Indian and the petite Chinese girl kept up without trouble.

Amber, meanwhile, was scarlet-faced and gasping. She had clearly never done any sort of physical training before—undoubtedly her years in Special Ed had exempted her from any PE classes. When Tristan gave her a reassuring smile, she made a face at him.

By the end of the class, Tristan doubted he would be able to walk back to the cafeteria. Waiting his turn at the water fountain, he sagged against the ice wall, scrubbing sweat from his forehead.

"Do we do this every time?" Tristan asked a fellow student.

"No," he said. "Sometimes we go running outside."

Tristan groaned.

Once again, no one talked at lunch. This time, Tristan wondered if the students had been trained into silence, or if they were simply as exhausted as he was. Over his lumpy, weak fish soup, he tried to imagine what it would be like to grow up here. Some of these kids had never known anything else. And if they hadn't experienced the outside world, they were likely to believe everything Ilana told them without question.

He found he pitied them.

Magic lessons followed lunch, this time with Ilana leading the class. To Tristan's surprise, they were not using marbles—instead, every spell they performed drew from their internal magic.

"Wouldn't it be safer to use marbles?" Tristan asked. He could see no downside to fueling their spells with marbles, while the opposite had the potential of harming them greatly.

"Our base here is relatively new," Ilana said sharply. "We don't have the luxury of drawing from a centuries-old cache of magic, so we need to conserve every marble we create. Every single one goes to fueling the globe. We use electricity for our lighting and cooking, as you've undoubtedly noticed, and train ourselves until we are fit enough to draw on our internal stores of power without detriment."

Tristan was so drained that he couldn't summon up even the faintest flicker of magic, and Amber was having just as much trouble. Ilana looked disappointed at their failure, though she did not comment on it.

Afterwards, they had a two-hour supervised study session in the cafeteria, during which they were meant to practice the spells they had learned during the previous class and complete a set of homework on theory. Tristan spent the time reading the same sentence over and over again, trying his hardest not to nod off.

Dinner was a relief, though Tristan was desperate to sit with Amber and puzzle through what they'd seen that day. He kept glancing her way across the cafeteria, and a couple times she met his eyes and blushed. His face grew warm every time this happened.

After dinner, their division was on kitchen-cleaning duty; Tristan was almost unequal to lifting the heavy pots and pans, so he took over the sweeping and mopping. He and Amber followed the rest of their division down the hall afterwards, both fighting to stay awake. It was an hour before curfew, according to his schedule, but he could think of nothing but sleep. He hoped the other students' bedrooms were more or less in the same direction as his, because he could not for the life of him remember the way.

Once five of the other students had disappeared into rooms along the main hall, Tristan cleared his throat and asked the last, the scrawny Indian boy who had somehow kept up with the workouts earlier that day, where his and Amber's rooms lay.

The boy gave him a surprised look. "Right here." He pushed open the door to Amber's room, and then Tristan's.

"Thanks," Tristan muttered. "What's your name?"

"Rajesh." The boy turned and retreated into his own room without another word.

These students were very strange. From what Tristan had seen so far, the classes appeared normal enough, but there must have been something more happening here, or they wouldn't act so lifeless.

Limping into his room, Tristan collapsed on his bed. He pulled the schedule from the bag he'd been given and tried to make sense of it, eyes glazing over. It was several minutes before he realized that, aside from three two-hour blocks of free time on Friday, Saturday, and Sunday, he would be busy from eight in the morning to eight at night every day.

A soft knock sounded at his door, so quiet he might have imagined it.

"Yes?"

"Can I come in?" Amber asked timidly

"Please," Tristan said. He had been wanting to talk to her properly all day. He leaned against the head of his bed while Amber sat cross-legged at the foot.

"What do you think?" he asked. "There's definitely something weird about this place."

Amber nodded. "All the students act like I did at the beginning of my first year."

"I hadn't thought of that!" Tristan smiled briefly. "I can't tell if they don't think for themselves, or if they're too scared to talk."

"Maybe it's a bit of both," Amber said. "Maybe they

were beaten into submission when they were young, and now that they are older, they've lost their independence."

Tristan hugged his knees. "That's a good point. We haven't seen any little kids, have we? If they're adopting babies, where are they all?" After the strangeness of the day, he wanted nothing more than to take Amber into his arms and cling to her.

"Should we do anything yet?" she asked.

"Not yet. First we need to watch and wait. They have to trust us before we try anything."

"Do you think they'll let us use their globe?"

Tristan grimaced. "I hope not. But we'll need to, eventually. I just hope they don't force us to do something horrible first."

"I bet they will," Amber said quietly. "That sounds exactly like the sort of thing Ilana would do. We will have to prove we can follow her orders blindly. We might have to destroy something major."

"And you'll do it, if they ask you to?"

"It's what the professors sent us here for. To prevent the destruction of humanity at whatever cost."

"At whatever cost," Tristan repeated blankly. "What if I can't do it? What if I'm too damn scared?"

Amber crawled forward and grasped Tristan's hand, her fingers warm on his numb skin. "You're incredibly brave. You would not be here otherwise." She gave him a sad smile. "I trust you more than I trust myself."

Tristan slept as though dead, his utter exhaustion fueled by physical weariness and jetlag. It took a while before he heard the knocking on his door in the morning, and longer still before he registered the sound enough to sit up and mumble, "I'm coming!"

Blearily he pulled on his uniform and boots and fetched his book-bag, stopping at the bathroom to splash water on his face. He knocked on Amber's door and waited for her to join him before turning in the direction of the cafeteria. There were no helpful students to guide them today, and Tristan's heart sank as he realized that the entire school looked the same—rounded white tunnels with white doors at regular intervals.

They turned left down a hallway Tristan thought he recognized, and by the time they had taken two more turns in what he assumed was the direction of the cafeteria, he and Amber were hopelessly lost.

"This is useless," he said abruptly, kicking another one of the blank white doors where the hallway dead-ended.

"Do you remember the way we came?" Amber asked.

"No. You?"

She shook her head. "Any marbles left for an Intralocation spell?"

Tristan dug in his pockets, but there was nothing to be found. Of course not—the filthy clothes he'd arrived in had vanished, and the three marbles remaining in those pockets were probably sitting beneath this school's globe by now.

Turning back, they tried to retrace their path to their bedrooms. Before long the hall narrowed; they definitely had not come this way before.

"We're in trouble," Tristan muttered, turning once again. He pushed open the door to his right and then the one on his left, neither of which led anywhere useful. "Damn it." Faster now, he and Amber retraced their steps up the hallway once again, pausing to glance in every room they passed. When the hallway forked, they chose the left corridor, hoping it would take them closer to the dining room.

"We'll probably just starve down here," Tristan said.

"Unless Ilana thinks we've come here to cause trouble," Amber said, pausing with her hand on a door. "This one is locked."

Tristan sighed. "At least we can eliminate that direction."

Heartbeat quickening, Tristan pushed open another door, and another. He wanted to give up, to sit down and wait for someone to find them, but he was afraid of getting caught where they didn't belong.

Throwing open the next door for a cursory look inside, he froze.

Someone was huddled against the wall, wrapped in blankets, one ankle fastened to the wall by a pair of heavy chains.

"Do you think they're dangerous?" Tristan whispered, beckoning Amber to the doorway.

She stared openmouthed at the hunched figure. "Professor?"

A second later, Tristan recognized the thin face and auburn hair.

It was Professor Merridy.

No, not "Professor" any longer. Tristan tiptoed into the room, his heart pounding. "Merridy? What's happening here?"

Merridy sat up abruptly, eyes wild. "Tristan! You have to get out of here! What on earth are you doing with these magicians?"

Tristan knelt gingerly beside Merridy, half-frightened that she would attack him. She did not seem to be in her right mind. "What've they done to you?"

Merridy wrapped the blankets closer about her shoulders. "They found me," she whispered. "They tracked me down and captured me. Those poor kids, too. They're here somewhere."

"It *was* you!" Tristan said, realizing suddenly what had happened. "Last summer. You told them where Zeke and I lived, and they tried to kill us."

Merridy nodded, not meeting his eyes. "They tortured me. Said they'd hang those beautiful twins. But I never told them where the Lair was."

So she had retained some sense of loyalty—or love—for Alldusk. "They found us anyway," Tristan said. He found he didn't blame her, though.

"Will you make sure the kids are okay?" Merridy asked weakly. "I don't think I'll live much longer. I don't want to abandon them."

Tristan swallowed. "You'll be okay, Professor." He still thought of her as his teacher.

Sitting up straighter, Merridy grabbed his wrist. "You

and Amber need to leave. Now. They'll kill you if they find you here."

"We're lost!" Tristan said. "I don't know how to get back to the school."

"What are you doing here, anyway?" Her grip on his wrist tightened.

If she was behind the attack on his mother's house, she couldn't be trusted to keep a secret. "We didn't want anything to do with Professor Drakewell," Tristan said. "He's evil. Ilana offered us a way out, so we left."

"I may have been wrong," Merridy said softly. "Drakewell was the lesser of two evils."

"Too late for that now," Tristan snapped. "We're here, and there's no going back."

Merridy put a hand on Tristan's shoulder. "You really have to get out of here. But it was nice to see you again. Some days I think I'm about to lose my mind."

There was so much more Tristan wanted to know, but he knew Merridy was right. Someone would notice their absence soon. Standing, he turned to the doorway.

Amber was not there. In two rapid strides, Tristan left the room, yanking the door shut behind him.

"Well. What have we here?" Ilana's quiet voice was dangerous. "Your little friend tells me you lost your way."

Amber was pinned to the wall behind Ilana, her wrist trapped in Ilana's slender fingers.

Tristan's heart leapt to his throat. "We *were* lost," he said quickly. "I think we turned too soon. I thought we were heading for the dining room, but then we hit a dead end, and we couldn't find the way back."

"Then what were you doing, speaking to Darla with such kindness?"

"All last year, I thought she was helping you," Tristan said. "I wondered if we were going to see her here. Did she do something wrong? Why was she down there?" He realized he was babbling, and shut his mouth with a snap.

"Oh, yes," Ilana said, still in that soft, deadly tone.

Tristan glanced at Amber, not sure what to do.

"What was that saying?" Ilana took Tristan's wrist in her other hand, almost gently. "Leopards can't change their spots? I think you need to come with me."

Heart pounding, Tristan fell into step behind Ilana. She could kill them without a second thought. Or she could torture them until they told her the truth. Then she could pick off everyone at the Lair, one by one. *Forgive me, Leila.*

"This way," Ilana said, opening yet another of the featureless side doors. "I have something to show you." She dragged Tristan and Amber in and slammed the door behind her. Two sets of manacles trailed from the wall; silently Ilana chained Amber's ankles to the wall before moving on to Tristan. Neither of them resisted.

"You're far too valuable to kill," she told them, stepping back to admire her handiwork. "But I don't trust either of you. I might give you a while to think things over, and once that's done, you can have another chance. You will have to prove your loyalty, though. And I am not a gullible woman. Enjoy yourselves." With a cold smile, she tucked the key into her pocket and left with a swirl of musty air.

The room was lit dimly by a single bulb on the ceiling, and the ice-carved walls radiated cold.

"Damn it," Tristan moaned, sliding to the floor. The band around his ankle pinched his skin as he moved. "We didn't even last two days."

"She said she hasn't given up on us," Amber said dubiously. "But we won't get away easily next time."

"Do you think she's recording us?"

Amber's eyes widened. "I hope not."

"Let's test it," Tristan whispered. Raising his voice, he said, "I wonder if Ilana found that bomb we planted? If she doesn't find it tomorrow, it's going to go off. And we're going to be screwed."

"I hope she comes back so we can tell her," Amber said, catching on quickly.

"I guess we're just sitting here waiting to die, then."

Tristan crossed his arms and leaned against the wall, which immediately began draining warmth from his core.

Now they just had to wait. There was still a chance that Ilana would change her mind and accept that their blunder had been just that—an accident. Tristan wasn't going to jeopardize that slim hope by saying anything incriminating if Ilana was listening.

Amber made a face at him and took a seat, resting her cheek on her knees.

That day was one of the longest Tristan had ever known. He didn't know whether they would be tortured or starved or just ignored; the worst part was the uncertainty.

The light did not change, nor did the temperature. He could only tell that time had passed when his stomach began growling.

"I'm starving," he said. "Are you?"

Amber nodded sullenly. "I can't feel any magic down here, either. The only power is mine and yours. It's so empty."

"Do you think she's planning to starve us?"

"Not if she actually wants to use us for anything," Amber said. "Remember the strength training? We would be less than useless if we lost our strength."

"Maybe she doesn't want our magic," Tristan said. "Maybe she just wants to torture us for information." He slammed his fist on the ice floor in frustration. "But we don't know anything that Merridy doesn't know! Why keep us alive at all?"

Amber did not answer.

Doubts began welling in Tristan as the hours stretched on, questions of loyalty and morality. Who was he doing this for, anyway? For two years he had followed Drakewell's orders, despite hating and mistrusting his headmaster; was he losing his own free will, or would he have done this even without Drakewell's instructions?

Either way, Ilana needed to be stopped. Anyone could see that.

But when had Tristan's hesitance morphed into a willingness to cause whatever destruction was necessary in this dangerous game?

He hardly recognized himself.

Eventually Tristan fell into a doze. How much later he could not tell, the door scraped open to admit Ilana. The smell of food was what hit Tristan first—rich, cheesy French onion soup in two deep bowls.

"Why are you here?" Ilana asked quietly. "Have you come to destroy us? Or to save poor Darla Merridy? Because you're too late for that. Your professor is dead."

Tristan went cold. They had just spoken to her hours ago, and now—

"Tell me. I want to hear a good story."

Tristan couldn't think. He was struck with an image of Merridy lying on the icy floor of her prison, eyes wide open, reaching out for something she would never have.

When Alldusk heard—

"We told you the truth," Amber said. Tristan tried to focus, silently praising Amber for stepping up when he had failed. She pulled up her left sleeve and showed Ilana the rope-burn. "Drakewell was furious after we used the globe without consulting him first. He tied us up belowground and threatened to kill us. That was when we realized our school was being run by a madman. We had to leave."

"Very well," Ilana said. "And is that the same story you would repeat if only the truth would save you from unimaginable pain?"

"Of course," Amber said, sounding hurt.

Ilana lowered the soup bowls, giving them an even better smell of the rich onions. "In that case, will you be so kind as to describe the protective wards currently surrounding your precious Lair?"

Tristan almost looked at Amber for support, but he caught himself just in time. "We don't know about all of them. Mostly they've got Prasidimums everywhere, and they fixed that big dome you shattered last year. I think it's weaker than before, though." He wouldn't mention the woven net of branches that they had enchanted just before Christmas; with any luck, it was a spell none of Ilana's magicians would recognize.

"Lies," Ilana hissed. "There is something new. That school has recently been camouflaged. It is no longer visible to outsiders."

"I didn't know that," Tristan protested.

Ilana turned the two bowls of soup over, splattering their meal all over the smooth ice. "Enjoy your meal." Eyes flashing, she left, slamming the door behind her.

"Well, I don't think she's recording us," Amber said weakly.

"Great. Just wonderful." Tristan crawled forward, unable to feel the hard floor on his numb knees, and pried a melted glob of cheese from the ice. The broth was already freezing solid. Amber copied him, grabbing sodden hunks of bread and translucent onions from the floor and eating ravenously. When Tristan had salvaged all he could from the wreckage of their dinner, he sat back on his heels, licking broth from his fingers.

His stomach felt even emptier than before.

Chapter 4

Ilana's Test

What felt like hours later, Tristan was lying on his side, curled up to preserve as much warmth as possible. The light was still on, and he could not sleep. When he glanced over at Amber, he could see his reflection in her forlorn eyes.

"You can't sleep either?"

She shook her head.

"Do you think you could break out of these?" he asked.

"Definitely. But she would never trust us again if we did."

Tristan nodded sullenly. "And then she'd kill us for sure."

"Sometimes I hate Drakewell for sending us here," Amber whispered. "I never wanted to play a role in something this important."

"You don't hate him because he's sent us here to die?" Tristan asked, incredulous. Their chances of success were so slim it was laughable. He would have stood a better chance against a lightning bolt.

Amber made a face. "I don't know what else I could have done. I have no other place, not in this world."

Tristan knew how she felt. If the Lair was destroyed, what then? Returning to civilization, to a landscape bled dry of magic, would be torture. This world was irrevocably his now. "I just wish we could have said goodbye," he muttered.

Amber crawled as close to him as her chains would allow, and Tristan was struck with a fierce yearning to hold her again. This was nothing like what he had felt for Evvie; in place of awkwardness and uncertainty, he felt such an overpowering, giddy affection that he almost forgot where they were.

Every nerve on fire, he shifted closer to Amber so he could press his shoulder against hers. Their heads rested together, and he reached on impulse for her hand.

And though Amber was so enigmatic he could rarely guess her thoughts, he knew exactly what it meant when she twined her fingers through his and held tight.

"You want to know something?" he said hesitantly.

"Mm?"

Tristan glanced sideways at Amber, whose eyes were closed.

"There's no one I would rather have here with me right now."

Her eyes flew open. "What about all of your friends? Didn't you leave anyone behind when you came to the

Lair?"

He shook his head, mouth twitching. "You must think I'm a lot cooler than I actually am. But I was always that lame kid who didn't know how to make friends. I thought it'd be a lot worse, after what Juvie was like, and after—" he gestured at his scars. "But it's not true. I was actually happy at the Lair, and—"

"I was, too," Amber said unexpectedly.

"I guess we both just—"

A sudden crash echoed down the hall outside, followed by a chorus of shouts.

Tristan and Amber flinched and sprang apart.

The moment of warmth fled as quickly as it had come.

"If Ilana found us like this, she would use it against us," Amber said softly.

Tristan cursed. "I know." Edging still farther away, he curled up again and reached out for Amber's hand.

She squeezed his fingers and gave him a grim smile. "At least we're not alone."

Tristan swallowed. He wished they could return to the days they had spent hiking through the Rockies, silent and determined as they crossed the barren expanse, huddled together at night.

Now they were left with nothing but a desperate longing to survive.

Tristan clung to Amber's hand even as her eyes dropped closed and her breathing grew quieter. At long last, he drifted off to sleep as well, his dreams punctuated with shadows.

* * *

He woke, disoriented and frozen stiff, to Ilana's voice.

"Good morning." Her silky voice spelled danger. "I trust you've slept well."

Neither Tristan nor Amber responded.

"No? That's a real shame." Ilana closed the door behind her. "The rest of my students slept soundly, tucked away in their warm, comfortable beds. It's such a shame you threw away your chance at a better life."

"You're not going to give us another chance?" Tristan asked, hugging his legs for warmth.

"I don't know. Should I? You have to prove that you want it. That it's more important to you than anything."

"How can we do that?" Tristan asked desperately. He was sure Ilana could hear his stomach rumbling from where she stood.

"You can do as you're told without complaining or asking questions," she snapped. "And when you're ready, you can tell us everything you know about the Lair."

Tristan opened his mouth to ask if they would get any breakfast, but he stopped himself just in time.

Just then, he noticed that Ilana was carrying a canvas bag, which she set on the floor in the middle of the room. "You each have two poached eggs and a slice of toast in here. They are hot, but they won't remain that way for long. Enjoy."

She turned and, with a swirl of her auburn hair, retreated.

"It's a trick," Tristan said, looking at the bag. "It has to be." He wasn't sure what to expect—had she poisoned the food? Or was a giant rat lurking in the bag?

Cautiously he crawled over and peeked inside. Instead of a plate, as he had expected, he saw a solid metal box, unadorned, with no obvious latch or lid.

"Damn it," he said as his stomach growled louder than ever. "It's a puzzle. I bet we have to open it with magic."

Amber glanced fretfully at the box. "I can't use magic down here. I have nothing to draw on."

"Can't we draw on our own power?"

"I'm not very good at that," she said sadly.

Tristan carried the box back to the wall, where they both stared at it for a long time, unspeaking.

"This sucks," Tristan said. "I don't even know how to begin getting at it. Unless we're meant to melt the box, or blow it up or something. And I definitely can't do that."

"Do you think we could melt a piece of it together?" Amber asked hesitantly.

"Might as well try. You do the spell, and I'll try to—to send you power, like we did with that barrier over the Lair."

Amber nodded. Tristan reached for her hand without a clear idea of what to do. Back in the Lair, they had each drawn the power from a single marble into themselves and sent it along to Drakewell, who had activated the barrier spell with the combined power of everyone at the school. Here, though, Tristan had to reach inside for his own power—something he had only done a few times before, and always by accident.

Closing his eyes, he tried to grasp ahold of any faint

piece of magic he could sense; after a moment, he realized he had been daydreaming about the steaming eggs and buttered toast. Shaking his head, he focused on the pressure of Amber's hand in his and tried to direct the heat of his body through his arm to that palm.

After a long time, his shoulder began to tingle, and warmth spread down his arm towards his hand. It was working! He concentrated the warmth into his hand and through to Amber, siphoning off as much as he could from his core. With a sudden jolt, the power left him. Tristan's head began throbbing, and he swayed.

The next thing he knew, Amber was slapping his cheek.

"Tristan! Wake up! You'll die on that cold ground."

"Calm down," he said, struggling to sit up. His head spun when he raised it from the ground. "I'm fine."

Amber's eyes were round and frightened. "Your pulse was so slow. I didn't know what to do."

"I messed up the spell, didn't I?" he said.

"It failed," Amber said, sitting back against the wall with her hands clasped on her knees. "Are you sure you're okay?"

Tristan nodded. "Don't worry about me."

"But I should," Amber said, studying him somberly. "Ilana should never have tricked us into trying that. It was very dangerous. Especially when we're exhausted and hungry."

"I'm just sad we don't get any food," Tristan said gloomily, slumping against the wall again.

Several more hours passed—or a lifetime, perhaps—before Ilana reappeared in the doorway. Her eyes immediately lit upon the metal box.

"You couldn't open it," she said flatly. "I'm disappointed. I expected better of Rowan's star pupils. Could you honestly not figure out such a simple spell?"

"I don't really know how to do magic without a marble," Tristan mumbled, feeling very small. Clearly the students here were miles ahead of him in that regard.

"Not even you, Amber?" Ilana's eyes flashed.

She hung her head. "I can't use my own power, not much. I usually draw on the network of magic hanging all around, but that only works outside, when there's enough life nearby. I had quite a lot of power in the forest outside the Lair."

Ilana's eyebrows raised just a bit; it seemed she was impressed in spite of herself. Tristan wondered why Amber had chosen to divulge such a dangerous piece of information—was she worried about what Ilana would do if she decided they were dispensable? "Well. This is an unacceptable shortcoming on your part. If you're going to help us at all, you have to learn to draw power from yourselves, and soon. It seems Rowan is so paranoid that he chose to limit your powers to keep you from causing any damage."

Tristan glanced at Amber in surprise. After two years of study, Drakewell still didn't trust his students? Or was it more of a general mistrust of magic in the hands of humanity as a whole?

"You will be less than useless without a command of your internal strength," Ilana said. "Starting this afternoon, you'll join the strength training classes—every one that takes place."

She knelt and put a hand on the metal box; a moment later one side fell off, revealing the plate of thoroughly cooled eggs and toast. "All you had to do was probe the box for weaknesses. There was a fragile clasp on the inside that had to be severed. That was all." Standing, she kicked the box towards them, toppling their breakfast onto the icy floor. "Eat up. You'll need all the energy you can get for weight training this afternoon."

When she left, Tristan and Amber descended on the cold eggs and soggy bread. It wasn't much, but it tasted like the best thing Tristan had ever eaten.

"I'm not going to survive strength training," he moaned when the eggs were gone. "I'll pass out again!"

Amber gave him a fleeting smile. "Don't worry. I'm even weaker than you."

They both fell into a doze, Tristan hunched against the wall, Amber curled around her knees.

When the door banged open a while later, Tristan jolted awake. This time it was not Ilana standing there but Stefan, who wore a strict frown entirely at odds with the jovial man he had seemed two days before.

"Are we doing strength training with you, then?" Tristan asked.

Stefan knelt to unlock their cuffs, not deigning to reply. Too happy about leaving their freezing cell to complain, Tristan fell into step behind him as they returned through the maze of passageways toward the gym. He was surprised by this new lack of security—had Ilana decided they were no longer a threat, given their inability to use magic underground?

They received several odd looks when they joined the class in the familiar gym, though no one spoke or showed undue interest. It seemed these students had been trained to act as puppets, to follow orders without question. Tristan wondered how many of them had been put through the same ordeal he and Amber were currently experiencing.

This time, the workout was entirely devoted to weight training. They lifted weights in endless repetition; Tristan and Amber each started with ten-pound dumbbells, while the rest of the class hefted twenty pounds and up; even so, he could hardly keep up. Long after his arms felt like they were about to drop off, they switched to medicine balls, which they held between their ankles while doing leg-drops and hugged to their stomachs for sit-ups. This time Stefan did not go easy on them. He walked around the class, barking out orders and reprimanding any student who got lazy or did a move sloppily. Tristan could barely manage to raise his back off the ground when they started doing sit-ups, so Stefan stood by his side and yelled at him until he sat up properly.

To his left, Amber was having even more trouble, though thankfully Stefan seemed to have chosen Tristan as his target this time around.

"Shoulders up!" he shouted. "Don't let the medicine

ball leave your stomach. *Tristan!* That's cheating. Ten more."

At long last, Stefan stepped back and said, "Class over. You have time to shower before dinner." He shot a look at Tristan. "Not you two. You must follow me."

His legs trembling, Tristan stood and limped after Stefan. Sweat had glued his shirt to his back, and his hair was pressed in damp strands down his neck. Amber followed, taking small, careful steps. As he had expected, they were led away from the cafeteria—which exuded the aroma of something delicious and roasted—and down the same hallway they had come from. After a week of this, they would at least be able to find their way to the cafeteria if they were ever allowed to go free, Tristan thought wryly.

After he locked them back into their shackles, Stefan drew a paper bag from his gym bag. "I've talked to Ilana," he said. "If you're going to build up strength properly, you have to eat."

"Thank you," Tristan said weakly.

Stefan didn't acknowledge him. Turning, he closed the door softly behind him.

"We can't keep doing this," Tristan said, ripping the paper bag open to reveal two tuna sandwiches and a sad, pale orange. "We have to tell her something." He took a big bite of the top sandwich before handing the second to Amber. "Something that won't hurt the Lair, but that will make it seem obvious we've given up on them."

"I know," Amber said. "I should tell them about the new barrier. I helped design it, you know. Without my help, they would take a long time to figure out its weaknesses and disable it before attacking the Lair. But I know exactly how it works."

"What are its weaknesses, then?" Tristan asked, an ominous feeling building in the pit of his stomach. The tuna sandwich was almost gone, and it had done nothing to fill the hole.

"The barrier is woven from branches and roots. It holds an illusion spell, and an overall protection spell. But the barrier only serves to ward off spells aimed at the Lair as a whole. It is a latticework frame, and if multiple spells were flung at it, one would go through."

"Wouldn't it guard against disasters sent from the globe?"

"Some. I suspect if we copied their hailstorm, the hailstones would get through easily. Provided the inner barrier was disabled as well."

"And how do we get rid of the inner barrier?"

Amber shrugged. "They managed it before, so I guess they could figure it out again."

"With a month's worth of rainstorms," Tristan said darkly. "My god, I can't believe we're upset that we can't figure out a way past their defenses."

Amber gave him a level stare. "We have to play this right."

"I know."

"And speaking of the inner barrier, wasn't there a tiny piece missing from the glass dome when we put it back on the globe?" she asked.

Tristan thought back to the day they had finished reassembling the puzzle-like shards of glass. "I suppose so. Drakewell might have found it, though. But you're right—I don't remember anyone finding that last piece. So…"

"I don't know where the missing piece is on the dome," Amber said hesitantly. "But I might be able to find it. I think I should try."

"How?"

"I don't entirely know."

It was a slim hope, but Tristan supposed it was better than nothing.

That night, Tristan was roused from a heavy sleep when the door clanged open. It was a moment before he remembered where he was, though the ache in his neck was reminder enough.

"Up," Ilana snapped, kicking Tristan and Amber with her heavy fur boots. Tristan recoiled from her foot, squeezing his eyes shut in hopes that she would go away.

When this failed, he rubbed his eyes and struggled to sit up, his ribs aching from where Ilana's toe had bruised his already-tender muscles. His legs barely supported him when he stood.

"Hurry!" she ordered. "Lazy, good-for-nothing leeches. Get up this instant!"

Amber stood, shaking, and stared at Ilana. Tristan was surprised to find that nothing stopped him when he took a step towards the door; clearly Ilana had unbolted their shackles before waking them.

All thoughts of telling Ilana about the barrier around the Lair fled Tristan's mind as he staggered after her, his legs protesting with every step. They couldn't have slept more than three hours; his head ached, his eyes felt dry and itchy, and every muscle spasmed when he moved.

"Where—" Tristan began, then stopped short. Ilana did not want them asking questions.

They stumbled up the icy hallway, past three doors, and up the ladder leading to the snow outside. The wind had died, and the stars were overwhelmingly bright overhead, an embroidered curtain of light. As they started across the ice, Tristan shot a questioning look at Amber, who shook her head, looking just as bewildered as he felt.

It seemed they walked for hours, the sky unchanging overhead, no landmark betraying their progress across the unblemished sheet of ice.

At long last, when Tristan's mind had gone blank from exhaustion and cold, Ilana stopped.

"Go," she said, her tone icy. "You're free. Leave this place and never return. You're not wanted here."

"But—" Tristan began, struggling to make sense of what she had said.

"Get out of here. *Now.*"

Without another word, Ilana turned and started back across the ice. Before long her figure had disappeared in the murky darkness.

Chapter 5

The Seminar

W-what's going on?" Tristan was shivering, the wind slicing across his skin and burrowing beneath his thin coat.

"It must be another test," Amber said. As usual, the cold did not seem to bother her. "We don't know what might be facing us if we return. If we had any doubts whatsoever, we would turn and leave that place behind."

"But we w-won't?" Tristan asked.

Reaching out, Amber grabbed his hands and sent a shock of warmth through Tristan. His shoulders sagged as the heat flooded through him, thawing his hands and jolting his feet back to life. "She might track us down and kill us if we leave. I could probably fight her off, but what would we accomplish then?"

"You're saying we should go back."

"We hardly have a choice," Amber said quietly.

Tristan thought longingly of his friends back at the Lair. Rusty would be hanging out with Eli and Trey now, and Leila…. Tristan was afraid she wouldn't forgive him if he returned. She didn't know the truth; she would suspect him of abandoning the Lair and then slinking back when he learned that betrayal came at too high a price.

"You're right," he said at last. "We can't give up now. But—" He didn't know how to say it, but this was the hardest decision he had ever made. Even harder than leaving the Lair in the first place.

This was their last glimpse of freedom.

"You're the brave one, not me," he said sadly. He would have given anything to turn away and leave that wretched prison far behind.

Tentatively Amber reached out and took his hands again. He drew her into his arms, seeking her comfort and her warmth.

"Why do you like me?" she whispered, her face against his shoulder.

The wind was riffling his hair, yet he felt impervious to the cold. "Because you're the most incredible girl I've ever met," he said. "Why do you like *me*?"

Amber gave a soft sniff, and Tristan realized with a start that she was crying. "Because—because you're the only person who has ever seen me as an equal."

Tristan drew away from her, taken aback by the stark vulnerability of her words. The stars were reflected in her beautiful eyes.

He wiped the tears from her cheeks with his thumb, pausing with his hand cupping her chin. How could anyone overlook her beauty? She was ethereal, like one of the fey folk—stunning in the way the moon and the stars were beautiful.

Hesitating, he brought his face closer to hers, hopeful and nervous. When his lips met hers, a shock ran through him like a spark. He thought Amber might flee, but her lips parted and their kiss deepened. As his lips moved with hers, Tristan knotted his fingers through her windswept hair.

Amber was smiling when they broke apart, her cheeks flushed in the starlight.

"Now we have a secret Ilana can never take," Tristan said, grinning back at her. Nothing else seemed to matter in that moment, not Ilana or her globe or her mindless disciples. Nothing mattered but Amber.

As they turned back towards Ilana's ice-cave, he took Amber's hand in his. He saw himself and Amber differently in that moment, two criminals who would forever stand out in a crowd, both lost and directionless until they had stumbled into this terrible, exhilarating world of magic. And he also saw how lonely it must have been for Amber. Before this, she had always been seen as the pitiful blind girl in Special Ed; now she was so talented she intimidated most of the other students at the Lair.

"Do you think we'll be able to make a difference?" Tristan asked as they retraced their path across the ice. He wanted to show her without words that he saw her for herself, that he loved her because of her individuality, but he didn't know how. "Are they ever going to let us near their globe?"

"I think they will," Amber said, her head tilted up to

the Milky Way. She watched the stars with a look of hunger, the myriad pinpricks of light reflected in her eyes. "I think they need our help. Maybe they suspect we know how to collect air magic."

"I don't know how," Tristan said, glancing sideways at her. "I'm not that useful."

"Not that dangerous, you mean," Amber said quietly. "They must never find out how powerful I am. They would enslave me."

Tristan gave her hand a brief squeeze. "You're stronger than them. They won't be able to hurt you."

"I hope you're right," Amber said wistfully.

As the night grew colder still, the wind fiercer, Tristan slipped into memories of the Lair; it was the only way to ward away the discomfort and forget the decision he'd made. Clouds began darting in wisps across the starry heavens, and a slivered moon rose above the flat horizon.

While the wind lifted his hair and swept a low cloud of snow across the ice, Tristan thought of the times they'd baked cookies with Quinsley and stayed awake late into the night by the Subroom fire. He remembered that terrible night after they had visited Whitney, when everyone had gathered by the fireplace in the Aspen Lodge to seek solace in one another. He had fallen asleep beside Leila, her warmth reminding him that he was not lost, that his life hadn't ended with the sight of that wretched, charred village.

And now…what would they be called upon to do for Ilana? Would they lay waste to a hundred villages like

Millersville? Would they ravage entire civilizations?

Tristan had the awful feeling that nothing waited for him after Ilana's school. He would die here, or remain trapped forever; there was no future beyond this. And it no longer mattered whether his friends could forgive him.

He would not be able to forgive himself.

Before long, Amber changed course, turning ever so slightly to the right. Tristan had no idea where they were going, but he assumed she knew. The Big Dipper hung before them, the North Star beckoning them forward.

"Not far now," Amber said, her voice ripped away in a gust of wind.

Tristan cursed. "I can't believe I'm doing this."

Amber shook her head. "Me neither. But I'll be here with you. To the end."

Tristan gave her a shaky smile, holding her hand tighter than ever. Now he could see the trapdoor, the edge outlined faintly in the moonlight. He knelt and lifted the ice-carved door. Then, taking a deep breath, he led the way down the ladder.

A weight of despair settled on him as soon as his feet touched the floor of the tunnel.

This was it.

Amber had barely joined him in the tunnel, the darkness almost complete with the trapdoor closed, when a light appeared around the corner and grew steadily brighter.

It was Ilana, her sharp, regal face glowing in the light of a flickering lantern.

"Are you certain of your decision?" she asked.

"Yes," Tristan and Amber said together.

"Then welcome," Ilana said, her tone warmer than Tristan had ever heard. "You have proved yourselves tonight, and you'll soon have a chance to further demonstrate your loyalty. Was it truly so bad with Drakewell that you had no choice but to join me?"

Tristan nodded. "Like I said, he's completely unreasonable. I don't trust him, and he's hated me since I first got there. Besides, it seems like he was only controlling the Map Room because he had no other choice. But you— you do it because you actually believe in what you're doing."

"What praise," Ilana said with what sounded like genuine warmth. "And such a shame about Rowan. I loved him once, you know. Before he changed. He nearly killed me, and he didn't have the heart to stay with me when I was hurt."

"I'm sorry," Tristan said, pretending he was convinced with her story. Natasha had told him the truth—that Ilana had been in a coma for several months, and Drakewell had stayed by her side until the doctors believed there was no hope left.

"Come this way," Ilana said. "Your rooms have been readied. I'm sorry I doubted you."

"It's okay," Tristan said. After seeing how harsh Ilana could be, he didn't trust her newfound kindness. If she thought she could win their devotion with sweet words, she was sorely mistaken.

"Your classes will resume tomorrow," she said,

stopping outside the pair of doors Tristan recognized from their first nights in the ice cave. "Sleep well."

With a smile that didn't quite reach her eyes, Ilana turned and left them.

"Hah—sleep well," Tristan said in an undertone. "It's probably four in the morning already. We'll be awake in another hour or two."

"At least she's given us another chance," Amber said. "You were very convincing, you know."

Tristan grimaced. "What does that say about me, that I'm getting better at lying?" He suddenly thought back to Merridy, who had fooled them all. Now she was utterly alone, with no one to mourn her end. "Poor Merridy. I can't believe she's—"

Amber winced. "Goodnight."

After she had disappeared into her room, Tristan stood for a long time watching her closed door, the memory of their kiss replaying in his mind.

Tristan had barely fallen asleep when he woke with a start, the lights blinding overhead.

"Breakfast is in five minutes," Stefan's voice called from the doorway.

"I'm up," Tristan mumbled, pulling his blankets over his head. After the unrelenting cold of their prison, the warmth trapped beneath his heavy stack of blankets felt luxurious.

Someone must have explained their return to the other students, because no one looked Tristan's way when he made for the seat beside Rajesh in the cafeteria. Amber was already there, looking very small between two giant boys Tristan recognized from their division.

The smell of food distracted him from everything else. After days of eating almost nothing, he was ravenous. He piled his plate with roast potatoes and scrambled eggs and toast, too happy to care that the food was bland and overcooked.

When Tristan paused to gulp down water, Rajesh gave him a fleeting smile. "I'm surprised you're back. Kids don't usually return once they've disappeared."

Tristan froze. "What happens to them?"

"No idea."

Rajesh must have caught a look from one of the professors, because he straightened and quickly adopted a blank expression.

As they climbed the ladder after breakfast and made for the same glacial stream they had been harvesting before, Tristan wondered if all the students were as mindless as they appeared, or if they were simply afraid to speak out. If he could win their trust, they might be persuaded to help overthrow their teachers.

But how could he get the measure of them, with professors watching them at every turn?

Tristan observed the students closely that day, alert for any sign of unhappiness or dissent. He found none. Each worked with expressionless dedication, no flicker of emotion betrayed on their faces. Rajesh was no different than the others; he did not meet Tristan's eye when Tristan fell into step beside him on their way to the afternoon lessons, nor speak a word except when called on.

At least he was beginning to learn the names of his classmates. The two enormous boys were Blake, a blond, broad-shouldered Scot who would have made a good football player, and Ricardo, a curly-haired Italian without an accent—Tristan assumed he had been one of the adopted students. The tiny Chinese girl was Mei Ling, and the rather plain-faced blond girl with a strong accent he didn't recognize was Pavlina. The most inscrutable student was Ori, a chestnut-skinned boy with a soft American accent and black eyes. Tristan could not place him.

With his attention divided, Tristan had found it very difficult to concentrate on his lessons; he was given extra homework to make up for each question he answered incorrectly in his lessons, and was consequently the last to leave the cafeteria following their supervised study time.

Amber was waiting in his bedroom when he arrived, perched at the foot of his bed with a vacant expression.

"What is it?" Tristan asked softly, closing the door. After that night out on the ice sheet, he felt her presence as though she was a campfire burning in his room.

"The tenth of May is in six days," Amber said. "I've been counting."

Tristan stared at her in alarm, all thoughts of romance forgotten. He had completely lost track of the time.

"If Ilana wants us to attack the Lair, we have to do it soon."

Tristan nodded, sinking down onto his bed beside

Amber. "I've been thinking. Are the students all completely brainwashed? Or are they just scared to speak up?"

"A bit of both, I think," Amber said.

"But how do we figure out which students aren't brainwashed?"

"We must be patient. We have as much time as we need," Amber said. "As long as Ilana doesn't plan a full attack on the Lair—"

"Or start sending disasters everywhere," Tristan added grimly.

Amber bit her lip. "I doubt that will happen right away. I think she wants our complete loyalty first."

"So we'll just wait and see what happens?"

"Yes."

Tristan slouched back against the wall of ice. "I'm afraid something will go wrong if we wait too long. But I bet some of the other students would help us if we asked nicely enough."

"And some would report us."

"I know." He couldn't see any better way, though. How was he supposed to get the measure of their fellow classmates if every hour of their day was structured by supervised activities? How could he get past their empty, emotionless façades without drawing attention from the professors?

"At least we're not stuck in that rotten cell any longer," Tristan said.

"Thank goodness." Amber yawned and got to her feet. "I think I should get some sleep now." Just before she disappeared, she turned and gave him a mischievous smile that sent blood rushing to his head.

Five more days, Tristan thought as he rolled out of bed the next morning. How on earth were they supposed to arrange it so they attacked the Lair exactly on the tenth of May? If either of them suggested it, the whole thing would look like a setup. And if they didn't, Ilana was likely to spring it on them when they least expected it.

But Ilana was not at breakfast, and neither Stefan nor any of the students called attention to Tristan or Amber that morning.

At lunch, Tristan sat between Ori and Mei Ling—they were the least intimidating students in the First Division—in hopes that he could get a bit more conversation out of them.

"How long have you been here?" he asked Mei Ling in a low voice.

"Forever," she said flatly.

"What about you?" he asked Ori.

He gave Tristan a long look. "Seventeen years. Why do you care?"

"I'm just curious," Tristan said quickly. "Don't you guys ever talk?"

"When we're supposed to," Ori said, turning pointedly back to his plate. On Ori's other side, Rajesh shook his head almost imperceptibly.

Frustrated, Tristan picked at his sandwich. He missed Quinsley's meals—the bread here was soggy, the vegetables pale and flavorless. What had happened to these kids? Had someone beaten the life out of them when they were too young to protest?

Instead of another study session after lunch, the First Division followed Stefan down a narrow corridor that led deep into the ice cave.

"You don't have any marbles, do you?" he asked Tristan and Amber gruffly, stopping outside a round metal door that could have come off a bank vault.

They both shook their heads.

"Good. Ilana will murder you if you try anything here, understood?"

Tristan swallowed. He had a feeling he knew where they were.

When Stefan turned the combination lock and pushed the door open, Tristan saw that his hunch had been correct.

This was Ilana's globe. The weapon they had come here to destroy.

Tristan glanced sideways at Amber. He would have given anything if it meant she could use her full powers underground. If she could draw on the force of nature, she would be able to blow the globe to pieces where they stood. He was surprised Ilana had allowed them into this well-guarded chamber so quickly; she was undoubtedly convinced Tristan and Amber could not harm her globe.

Unfortunately, she was right.

Ilana's globe was smaller than the one in the Lair, just a foot taller than Tristan himself, and the continents were carved from what looked like rose onyx offset by a shiny black ocean, all of it much cruder than the globe he was accustomed to. There was only one table in this room, and with a shiver of apprehension, Tristan realized it was molded into the shape of a very familiar valley in Canada. Though the buildings of the Lair did not register on the granite surface, he could easily recognize the clearing where it sat.

"Tristan, Amber, stand back," Stefan said curtly. "Ilana does not want you touching the globe yet. Mei Ling, you're first today." Opening a trapdoor that Tristan had overlooked, he cranked a handle that raised a platform and sent a cascade of ten marbles clattering from one vault to another.

As Mei Ling stepped up, determination written into the lines of her forehead, Stefan relocated the disc to one of the islands of Hawaii and said, "I want a ten-marble eruption of Mount Kilauea. Remember to send the lava towards the village this time. And make sure you use ten marbles—anything less is just lazy."

Mei Ling took a glass quill from Stefan, identical to the one they'd used at the Lair apart from its lack of a silver air marble. Tristan felt a savage pleasure at the thought that Amber was the only magician alive who could harvest air magic.

The trapdoor was still open, and when Mei Ling began to draw the complicated gesture that triggered a volcanic eruption, the ten marbles in the vault beneath the globe vanished one by one. When she lifted the quill from the granite table, one marble still remained. She winced.

After a pause, the volcano on the table erupted on one side, the lava hazy and almost transparent on the map. A slew of burning rocks rained onto the nearby village, followed by an oozing tongue of magma that crept down the mountainside, stopping just past the first three houses, which went up in flames as soon as the magma curled against them.

Watching the chaos with a carefully blank expression, Tristan wondered where the people were. Why had no one fled the volcano?

Then he remembered that they couldn't see auras on this map. For all they knew, everyone might have escaped.

Or the entire village could be dead.

"You're one marble short," Stefan said dispassionately as the village continued to burn. "But it was better than before. And you're getting better at directing the lava."

He lifted the anchor and spun the globe west, repositioning the disc on an Asian country Tristan couldn't identify. "Ricardo, you'll be flooding a town near the eastern border of Bangladesh. Use eight marbles to send rain from each direction, and we'll check back on the results tomorrow."

The rest of the class continued in the same vein, though Pavlina and Ori were called upon to monitor the results of previous disasters rather than cause new ones. For those—a mudslide in New Zealand and a tidal wave in the South Pacific—Stefan pulled up a set of news articles on a laptop, from which he rattled off statistics and details.

"Ninety-four, Ori. Well done. No evacuations. But you

didn't use every marble, so that's a point down. Eight points." He turned to Pavlina. "The mudslide was badly timed. No casualties. And only four out of five marbles used. That's a zero."

Pavlina looked down at her feet.

Tristan felt thoroughly shaken by the time their class was dismissed. To his surprise, they had two hours of free time before dinner, so he followed the rest of the students back to their rooms.

"What are the points about?" he asked Rajesh in an undertone as soon as Stefan left their group.

"You need a thousand points to move up through each of the divisions," he said, "and seven thousand points to graduate."

"How many are you at?" Tristan asked, not entirely sure he wanted to know the answer.

Rajesh made a face. "Four thousand, eight hundred and fifty-seven. I'll get a badge when I pass five thousand."

Tristan didn't want to contemplate how many deaths that equated to. He hoped fervently that the points could be won some other way besides causing successful disasters. "And what happens after you graduate? Do you stay here, or go somewhere else?"

"Well, you met the first set of graduates who'd gone through the whole program. They were the ones watching your old school from that cave."

"Oh." Tristan suddenly felt guilty for his school's attack on the magicians. Ilana had forced them into that situation, with minimal training and no real-world experience, and treated them as expendable. "I guess you're not looking forward to graduating, then."

"No." Rajesh glanced backwards to see if anyone else was listening. "I think the rest of the graduates are just harvesting magic all the time. Oh, and a few are pretending to live normal lives so they can keep adopting new kids for us. Some of them are researching air magic, and the rest are just working. Brute labor. It's a bit sad that all our training amounts to that."

"Why don't you just hang back, then?"

Rajesh laughed humorlessly. "What, you mean deliberately fail my classes? I'd be dead before I could say 'it was an accident.'"

"Well, I guess the next few years matter, anyway," Tristan said. "Ilana's just saving you until she can mount a full-out attack."

Rajesh nodded grimly. They had reached their rooms now, and he paused with a hand on his doorknob.

"Are we all allowed in each other's rooms?" Tristan asked.

"I suppose. No one's forbidden it."

"Hmm. See you at dinner?"

"Of course." With a half-smile, Rajesh disappeared into his room.

Tristan followed Amber into her room, wondering what she had thought of their visit to the globe. More than anything he had seen thus far, their casual use of disasters had unsettled him. It was not just one headmaster who was required to sacrifice his morals; no, every student here was tainted by the globe's evil work, and he wondered how they justified it to themselves.

Maybe they didn't realize the full implications of what they did. If they had never been anywhere outside of this ice cave, the greater world would seem like an abstract concept, something irrelevant to their lives and work here.

"You okay?" Amber asked.

Tristan shook his head to clear it. "What?"

"You had a funny look on your face…"

"Sorry. I was just thinking about—about that globe. It's insane, isn't it?"

Amber nodded dully. "They will start asking us to use it soon. You saw how frightened I was last year. I'm not sure I can do it."

"You can always pretend you can't figure out how to do it right," Tristan said. "I'm sure you can 'accidentally' send the disasters off in the wrong direction so no one gets hurt."

"How long will they believe that?" she asked. "And how much longer before they launch the real attack?"

Tristan sighed. "Not much longer, I bet. I'll ask Stefan tomorrow."

Sitting cross-legged on the floor with his back against her bed, he pulled out a workbook with a set of homework problems they'd been given the day before. He had glanced at them briefly the previous night but, too tired to concentrate, had not given them much thought. Now he realized that the problems referred to the numbers of marbles of each variety involved in disasters of all magnitudes. A complex series of calculations was necessary for each—there was a separate equation for each type of disaster based on force, duration, and range desired.

"My god, this looks awful," Tristan said, squinting at the first equation. "Why didn't I pay better attention in Algebra?" It struck him that the disasters they had seen in the past hour had not been a display of haphazard destruction—they had been carefully calculated and planned down to the last marble.

Opening her own workbook, Amber wrinkled her nose at the problems. "I've never done a proper math class in my life. I think we might need private tutoring."

Tristan laughed. "With who? Ilana?"

Tristan had expected to wait until the next day before he saw Stefan, but after dinner that evening, he and the rest of the First Division were ushered out of the cafeteria and down a long staircase with metal steps embedded in the ice for extra traction. The lights dimmed as they went, until the students each grabbed a torch from its bracket and used for the final descent. Somewhere along the way—Tristan didn't notice where, since he had been focused on maintaining his footing on the slick stairway—the ice transitioned to rough grey bedrock, inlaid here and there with veins of black.

Though Tristan hadn't looked at his schedule before dinner, he had a feeling he knew exactly what they were doing. They were harvesting earth magic.

At long last, the stairwell ended in an unfinished hallway that was wider in some places and narrower in others. He followed the rest of the class in transferring his torch to a new sconce on this wall, where the flames lit the chamber with a shifting orange radiance.

As the six other students passed around a bucket of what looked like pickaxes, Stefan beckoned Tristan and Amber over. "We're aiming for crystalline structures here. Ordinary stone won't hold any magic. You'll notice the picks are hollow—once you've cracked a stone, hold the pick in place so the vapor floods right in. Then you can cap it off and trade for a new pickaxe."

"Why can't you just catch the vapor in a jar, like usual?" Tristan asked.

Stefan gave Tristan a stern look. "Earth magic is very hard to see, as it produces almost no light of its own. Now get to work."

It took a long time before Tristan began recognizing the crystals within the veins of black rock, some of which were smaller than the head of a pin, and longer still to break open his first faceted stone. When he did, he couldn't tell if anything had come out of the rock, so he tried to peer into the hollow pick.

"Cap it off, you idiot!" Stefan cried. "You will lose it that way!"

Tristan fumbled in his pocket for the cap, which he shoved onto the end of the pick. He still couldn't tell whether anything was inside the hollow chamber, but from Stefan's reaction, he guessed this form of magic was rare and precious.

Two hours later, they packed up their gear and headed

back up the endless staircase, sweaty and covered in dust. With a pang, Tristan imagined how ecstatic Delair would have been to learn all of this. Returning their torches to the wall, they tromped off to the showers in a silent pack. To Tristan's surprise, one of the boys started humming in the next stall over.

The following morning, as the First Division started across the ice towards their water magic-harvesting spot, a sheen of mist swirling about their ankles, Tristan caught up with Stefan and fell into pace beside the teacher.

"Hey, um…" He realized he didn't know how to address these teachers—did they insist on formality, or prefer that students addressed them by their first names? When Stefan did not so much as glance in Tristan's direction, he plowed on. "I was just wondering—why did you attack Haiti and Chile? Why not somewhere more important? New York City, or something."

Stefan glanced sideways at Tristan. "Do you really want to know?"

"Yeah."

"Fine, then." Eyes fixed on a far-off smudge wreathed in mist, Stefan said, "We're not ready to attack anywhere obvious yet. That's all there is to it. It's why we were so desperate to recruit new students, and why we need you and Amber.

"Haiti was our first large-scale disaster, so we contained it on an island just in case it caused more damage than we expected. Unlike your former school, we don't have an endless supply of marbles, so we wanted to target somewhere where our work would have a major impact.

"Well, it worked. The Haitian earthquake was more successful than we'd dreamed, so we decided to try something on a mainland continent. Chile was perfect, cut off from the rest of South America by the Andes so we could study it in isolation, and this time we managed to deal a serious blow to a country accustomed to natural disasters. We won't be ready to attack any major population centers for another couple years; when we attack London, Beijing, and New York City, we don't want them to get the chance to rebuild. We have to harvest enough power to target hundreds of cities throughout the world in one great string of disasters. If we don't, plenty of those countries are rich enough to recover and carry on. Which would defeat the purpose of what we're doing."

"Which is…wiping out all humanity so the earth gets a chance to recover?" Tristan said, repeating what Ilana had told them.

"Precisely. Though we intend to preserve a few human lives so we can start over again."

Fighting to keep his face blank, Tristan nodded. It sounded like Ilana was trying to enact some Noah's Ark scenario, where a few "chosen ones" survived while the rest drowned in the flood. How did she expect that to work? Whoever she selected to survive would be no kinder or more intelligent than the billions she planned to sacrifice in the process.

"It's funny," Rajesh said quietly from Tristan's left.

He jumped. "What?"

"All of Ilana's ideas are very reasonable, when you think about it. She's a firm believer in deep ecology, which is a great idea in principle."

"What's that?" Tristan asked.

"You'll hear *all* about it once we're done harvesting today," Rajesh said drily. "But the problem is, Ilana's a psychopath. Maybe someone could put her ideas into play and do it well, but not her."

"And the rest of the teachers?" Tristan whispered.

"My god, they practically *worship* her."

Tristan glanced back to see whether Amber had heard any of this, but she was trailing far behind the group. He assumed she was wary of being seen spending too much time with him.

They arrived at the stream for harvesting just then, which meant everyone had to huddle too close together for any conversations to continue undetected. Briefly Tristan wondered if any of the other students used their long daily walk as an opportunity to talk without being overheard. He expected they got tired of the monotony of the ice sheet, the never-ending glare of sun against snow. Right now, though, the entire landscape looked ethereal, bathed in rising swirls of mist.

An hour and a half later, after the haze had lifted and the ice gleamed in the morning sunlight, they returned to the school for something that was labeled on Tristan's schedule as "Seminar." He had no idea what that was about, though after what Rajesh had said, he was growing curious.

The more he learned about Ilana's school, the more conflicted he became. The lines between right and wrong were blurring more with every day—what the Lair did made sense because it sought to maintain a fragile sort of balance between civilization and nature, yet it was wrong because no humans should be allowed to decide who lived and who died. And Ilana's mission seemed reasonable as well, because even Tristan could appreciate that humans had done so much damage it would take an apocalypse to stop them, but the way Ilana killed with such precision and apathy chilled him to his core.

Stefan led them down a corridor on the right-hand side of the labyrinth, finally stopping at an enormous circular room with three tiers of benches ringing the center. Surprisingly, the room wasn't empty—Ilana waited on the innermost bench, a tall black teacher across the room from her, the dozen-odd students in his division perched on benches behind him.

Apparently this was a full-school seminar.

As Tristan's division filed into benches directly to Ilana's left, other students followed, taking their seats in a precise, orderly manner. The only sound came from the shuffling of footsteps, and as soon as everyone was seated, silence filled the room.

"Good morning," Ilana said. "Thank you for joining me today. On behalf of our two new students, I thought we might return to the basics and remind ourselves why we're all here."

Tristan's eyes flickered nervously to Amber, who sat two rows ahead of him. Though Ilana was facing away from Tristan, he imagined she spoke directly to him. "What are the five principles on which this institute was founded?"

Ilana pointed at Anton, the bearded pilot, who responded as though reciting from memory, "All life is inherently valuable—humans no more than anything else—and humanity is well on its way to destroying most of that life."

Ilana pointed to another teacher. "Unless something drastic happens, we're about to tip the earth past a point of no return. Our planet is quickly becoming too hot, too dry, and too extreme to sustain a wide diversity of life."

A third teacher: "Human overpopulation is more or less responsible for every issue facing us today."

Stefan was next. "We've got a responsibility to fix this. And us more than most, since we have the power to make a difference."

Ilana added the fifth and final principle. "We cannot do anything, within the bounds of today's political and economic spheres, that will make a difference. It's all too little, too late. The only *true* way to fix things is to drastically reduce the human population." She turned and gave Tristan and Amber a calculating look. "We're not the only ones who support this idea, you know. Others—scientists and philosophers and environmentalists—have come to the same conclusion. Some believe, as we do, that a complete collapse of the industrial world is necessary to allow regrowth."

Turning back to the center of the circle, she said, "What detrimental processes are in place that will not end until we solve our population crisis?"

This time, she began pointing at students for answers.

"Desertification."

"Acidification of the ocean."

"Accumulation of waste."

"Over-use of water, leading to drained aquifers."

"Global warming."

It went on like this, questions being answered by students throughout the room, for the rest of the hour. The worst thing was that a small part of Tristan agreed with Ilana. Her ideals were sound; it was just her method of achieving them that was despicable. He tried not to dwell on this, instead paying attention to the students who spoke. He had never spent time with anyone outside of the First Division before, and he was surprised to find that while the older students had accents from a hundred different places, anyone under the age of about twelve had a vague, lilting accent that wasn't quite European nor quite American.

When the hour was up, Ilana and her fellow teachers passed around a set of books and instructed the students to spend the next hour quietly reading Chapter 8. Tristan opened his book to the right page and pretended to read, though he was thinking hard. Did Ilana actually believe in everything she claimed to uphold? If she was really concerned for the environment, Tristan would have thought she'd be running some hippie commune that lived off the earth while gathering magic on the side.

Besides, if all lives were equal, why did six billion humans deserve to die?

Tristan had a funny feeling Ilana was just using this philosophy—deep ecology, or whatever Rajesh had called it earlier—to push her own aims. If he wasn't mistaken, she was more interested in getting revenge on Drakewell than on working towards a better earth.

He couldn't wait to talk to Amber and see what she had thought about the seminar. With their teachers supervising every minute of the day, he had to wait until the evening, when his division was released for one of its rare blocks of free time.

But on his way to dinner, someone grabbed his wrist and dragged him into a side room.

Tristan nearly shouted in alarm; then he remembered this school was filled with his enemies, none of whom would be disposed to help him.

The man who had grabbed him was burly, his neck covered in tattoos.

"I don't trust you, Tristan Fairholm," he spat, tightening his grip on Tristan's wrist. "Something about you smells...*funny*. You can bet I'll be keeping a close eye on you. One step out of line, and—"

He wrenched Tristan's wrist backwards. Tristan gasped in pain, terrified of the hungry look in the man's eyes.

"Run along, now. And be a good boy."

When the man released his wrist, Tristan fled, breaking into a run when he reached the main corridor. He thought he could hear laughter chasing him along.

Chapter 6

The Storming of the Lair

All through dinner, heart still thudding too fast, Tristan kept glancing over his shoulder to see if the tattooed man had followed him. The man did not join the others, though. Come to think of it, Tristan couldn't remember ever having seen him before.

After dinner, most of their division headed to a room filled with cushioned armchairs and tables, where they pulled out their homework and began working in silence. Blake and Ricardo started a game of ping-pong on the dented table at the back, throwing taunts and insults as they whacked the ball back and forth. They were both very good.

Amber was the last to poke her head into the room, eyebrows raised in surprise. She made for the corner where Tristan sat, dazedly watching Blake and Ricardo.

"I did not expect this," Amber said, settling into a deep armchair beside Tristan. "Ping-pong? And free time?"

Tristan nodded. "Hey, Amber. Have you ever seen a

big, scary guy with tattoos here?"

"No. Why?"

In a low voice, he recounted the man's threat.

Amber shivered. "What do you think he's doing here?"

"Nothing good. If I'd seen him in a city, I would've run as fast as I could in the opposite direction." He slumped back in his chair. "What did you think about that seminar?"

Amber was still watching Blake and Ricardo out of the corner of her eye, as though hypnotized. "I think there are a lot of very good people who believe the same things. But I think Ilana is not one of them. Nor are her teachers."

"Stefan doesn't seem too bad," Tristan said, though he agreed with her.

"Stefan was not brainwashed, not raised in this place. He came here of his own volition. I think he is much worse than he appears."

Tristan frowned. "What about the others, then? Is Rajesh just pretending he doesn't like Ilana so he can gain our trust? Is he going to betray us, too?" Rajesh was sitting at the opposite end of the room, smiling lopsidedly as he said something to Mei Ling, who regarded him in stoic silence.

"I don't think so," Amber said after a pause. She had torn her eyes from the ping-pong players at last. "There must be a reason he has turned on Ilana."

"Yeah." Tristan dug out a workbook, wondering if there was an unspoken assumption that he ought to be doing homework in his free time.

"Only three more days," Amber whispered. "What should we do?"

"Maybe we should just wait until next month," Tristan said. "I have no idea how we're supposed to do this."

Amber folded her arms. "Me neither. Oh, I wish I could go wandering again. I feel so trapped here. I'm afraid my power will just fade away if I stay here too long. I might forget how to use it."

"I'm sure you won't," Tristan said. "But I don't like it any better than you do."

Two hours later, the First Division filed off to bed in a tight group, conversations dying as soon as they left the room. Tristan went to bed with his head stuffed full of questions—who was the tattooed man? And how on earth would they persuade Ilana to let them attack the Lair in three days?

He lay awake for hours, trying desperately to think of excuses for attacking the Lair, but none occurred to him. Could he tell Ilana that Drakewell would be putting up a new barrier soon, so they'd have to do something before then?

No, because then she'd accuse him of withholding information. Could he just go to her and ask outright for permission to attack the Lair?

No, that would sound suspicious. She would know something was up.

Tristan slept badly that night, and dreamed that he was trying to fly a small plane through the barrier so he could bomb the Lair. Every time he approached, the plane just bounced off the barrier, while Drakewell stood in the meadow below and laughed at him.

He had just fallen into a proper, deep sleep when someone rapped on his door.

"Damn you!" Tristan yelled through his blankets.

According to his weekly schedule, this was Sunday morning, but it certainly didn't feel like the weekend. Back at the Lair, Sundays had meant a leisurely brunch with pancakes or French toast or cinnamon rolls, and a bout of enjoyable procrastination before Tristan and most of the other students tackled the homework they had put off.

Here, the weekend schedule was identical to the weekday schedule. Worse still, Tristan realized they were rostered for a toilet-cleaning session that afternoon. On a Sunday. *Ugh.*

Well, he supposed it would be better than getting locked in that cell again. And less painful than their strength training sessions.

Tristan got his chance to speak with Ilana sooner than he expected. They had a two-hour globe session just after lunch, and this time she took over the class, Stefan sitting at the back and taking notes.

Once again, Tristan and Amber were not allowed anywhere near the globe, though Ilana did ask them several questions. Tristan didn't know the answer to a single one. As Stefan made a note on his clipboard following Tristan's third incorrect guess, it struck Tristan for the first time just how badly prepared the Lair would be if anything went wrong. There were only eight professors, if you counted Quinsley, and most of them had never worked the globe before. If something happened to Drakewell or Natasha, the Lair would be left crippled. The other professors would do their best, but their knowledge of the globe was nothing compared to that of every student and teacher under Ilana's instruction.

Only a few months ago, Tristan had been revolted at the very idea of touching the globe. If his friends were to learn how to cause disasters, they would be forced to sacrifice some part of their humanity.

Was it worth it, in the name of protecting the Lair?

As the students were packing up their bags and leaving the globe behind, Tristan caught Ilana's eye. She beckoned him over with a long-nailed finger.

"How are you settling in?" Her smile was dangerous.

"Fine," he said. "This is all so interesting. We didn't learn any of those calculations at the Lair—how many marbles it takes for a certain disaster, or anything."

"That's because they assume—to their detriment—that their marble supply is infinite," Ilana said with satisfaction. "They will run out of air and water in a few years, I guarantee it. Oh, if only we could have a share of their remaining air magic."

"You're going to destroy the Lair someday, aren't you?" Tristan asked.

Ilana gave him a sharp look. "That's a rather grave assumption."

He tried not to betray his nerves. "Well, what if we

could steal their hoard of magic before the place was wrecked?"

"And what makes you think we wouldn't rather move into those luxurious quarters once the pests are gone?"

Crap. He shouldn't have said anything. "Never mind. Um…who was that man with tattoos all over his neck?"

Looking surprised, Ilana said, "That's Mordechai. He has a very special job here."

"He said he doesn't trust me," Tristan said, his pulse quickening. "Why not? I'd do anything to convince you we deserved your trust."

"Mordechai will be rather harder to convince than me," Ilana said drily. "But if you're ready, I want you and Amber to plan an attack on your beloved Lair. Would you agree to that?"

"Of course," Tristan said quickly. "But—I need to practice the equations a bit more first. Can we have a couple days to practice?"

"Next week, then," Ilana said with a satisfied smile.

"We'll probably be ready by Tuesday, if you want," he said.

"Very good. I'll speak with Stefan. Now, isn't there somewhere you're meant to be?"

"Cleaning stupid toilets," Tristan muttered under his breath.

Smiling smugly, Ilana swept away, leaving Tristan trying to catch his breath as his heart rate slowed.

He hated talking to Ilana. He could never tell what she was thinking.

Though Tristan was late arriving at the boys' toilets, he received nothing more than a frown from Stefan.

"The last four cubicles," he said, handing Tristan a rag and a spray bottle. "I want the floor clean enough that I could eat dinner off it."

As Tristan got to his knees and began scrubbing the tiles in the first cubicle, he contemplated the fact that life here was so devoid of happiness that there was no need for punishments. Just existing was punishment enough.

"I've done it," he told Amber triumphantly that night, following her into her bedroom. "Ilana's going to have us attack the Lair on Tuesday."

She smiled. "I thought that might have been what kept you. Now, how are we going to do this?"

"If you figure out where the hole in the enchantment is, I can send the disaster," Tristan said. "We're going to do another ice storm, right?"

Amber nodded vaguely. "Do you think we could 'accidentally' use up more marbles than we should?"

"It's dangerous," Tristan said, "but it might be our only chance to do something like that. Before long we'll be calculating all the exact details, and no one will believe us if we say we screwed up." The problem was, none of this helped with their ultimate goal of destroying Ilana's globe. Yes, they would hopefully gain her full confidence before long, but...then what? How could they get access to the globe outside of class?

The only ideas that came to him were digging through

the walls to the globe—which, given the fact that he still got turned around on his way to the cafeteria, had exactly zero chance of succeeding—or creating a diversion that would send everyone in the room running off while he and Amber remained behind. Their teachers weren't that stupid, though. They would never leave either of them in the globe room unsupervised.

"Imagine if we'd been spies at the Lair," he said wryly. "We had so many chances to do all sorts of damage! I was sick of those night shifts in the Map Room. If only this were that easy."

Amber nodded solemnly. "It does seem impossible, doesn't it? I wish Drakewell had given us a better idea of what to expect. Or sent us a bit of help."

"What, like a letter with instructions? That would go down really well with Ilana."

Amber laughed, though without much humor. "I just feel so isolated here. We can't trust anyone, not even Rajesh, and by ourselves we are so weak. I wish I could use my powers properly up here. I feel almost crippled without them."

"I know what you mean," Tristan said. He reached for her hand, feeling hollow inside. "I felt that way last summer. I'm not as good at sensing things as you are, but...there weren't any auras at my mom's house, not that I could see, and everything was just so bleak and empty. I missed it so much that I started looking for any scrap of nature I could find."

"Why did you go home, then?"

Tristan shrugged. "I felt like I owed it to my mom. But I think she'll be okay now. She's gotten back with my dad, and I think they might work things out." He hung his head. "It must've been hard for them, losing two sons at the same time."

Amber squeezed his hand, though she seemed at a loss for words. After a moment, Tristan shook his head and banished the memories. "So. I'm assuming it's just the longhouses that are going to be destroyed when we send the ice storm? Or do we have to smash the greenhouse, too?"

"Everything, if we want to be trusted," Amber said. "But they will have to believe us. We cannot see past that barrier on their map, remember?"

"Right." This was going to be very tricky.

Tuesday came far too quickly. Tristan still wasn't ready for this, not at all, and was almost certain he'd make a fool of himself in front of the class.

Ilana pulled Tristan and Amber aside at the end of dinner to fill them in.

"I know you won't be fully destroying the Lair. There are too many barriers in place for that, and we simply don't have enough power to get through them. But you somehow know a way to attack through the outer enchantments?"

Amber didn't meet Ilana's eyes. "Yes. There is a hole in the barrier, a piece we could not find when we were fixing it last year. I think I can get through that, if I manage to find it."

"Could you bring the barrier down again?" Ilana asked swiftly. "I believe it was down for several months the last time we shattered it."

"I don't know," Amber said. "But I will try."

"Very well. It will be an earthquake that destroys that Lair in the end, but for now, we don't have enough power for the magnitude we'll need. So today you will burn down every building in that meadow, and follow it by flooding the school."

Tristan swallowed. This was going to be much harder than the ice storm they'd planned. "Can we look for that weak spot, then? Before class?"

"Of course." Signaling to Stefan, Ilana led them briskly down the corridor of ice to the globe room.

"How did you manage to build this?" Tristan asked as he stopped before the roughly-hewn globe. "Drakewell couldn't have done it."

"I know that," Ilana said with satisfaction. "You know, Europe had a globe before North America did, though it's long since been destroyed. China had one before it, and Egypt before that. But we dug up the records our European magicians had left, and followed the same method they used. Their globe was constructed in Italy during the Renaissance, but the magicians who inherited it were divided in a political tussle that eventually destroyed them. The survivors fled to North America."

"Are there any magicians left in Europe?"

"Not that I'm aware of," Ilana said. "We've gone to great lengths trying to track down anyone who was associated with the old magicians' guild, but it seems most of them died or left the continent without passing down their knowledge. Now, how do you intend to find this weakness in the barrier?"

Tristan blinked and returned his attention to the globe. To his right, Amber affixed the disc to a blank section of Canada, which quickly resolved into the mountains surrounding the Lair. Standing beside the table, she took the glass conduit from Ilana and studied the empty meadow.

"This would be so much easier with a bit of air magic," she whispered. With a slow, graceful gesture Tristan didn't recognize, she conjured up a layer of fog that hung low over the valley. While Ilana's attention was focused on the swirling fog, Amber reached in her pocket and stealthily slipped a silver air marble into the glass conduit. Tristan stared at the glass quill in disbelief. She must have harvested that on her own.

With the help of the air magic, Amber sent a breeze that pressed the fog lower into the valley, forcing it as close to the dome as it could go. Most of the fog settled around the dome, not penetrating the barrier, but in one corner it began swirling like bathwater down a drain.

"That's the gap," Amber said, pointing at the funnel. "If we work through that, we should be able to attack the lair directly."

Ilana's eyes widened. "Very well done, Amber. Just incredible." Tristan didn't like the greed lurking behind her amazement.

Flushing, Amber dropped her hands. With a glance at the conduit, Tristan saw that the silver marble had vanished. Its power was exhausted.

"And now, should we wait for the rest of the class to join us before the main show?"

Tristan nodded, studying the lingering cloud of mist. If he guessed correctly, the hole in the barrier sat directly above the longhouse where Gracewright kept her indoor garden. That would be the first to go, unfortunately; he hoped she'd had the foresight to remove her precious plants before joining the others in the forest. Though it was evening here, it would be sometime around midmorning at the Lair. He prayed that everyone had enough time to leave.

At least the flood wouldn't be able to get past the stairwell. Would it?

"Rain should go through the barrier, right?" Tristan said.

"Unless your headmaster has put up a new barrier, then yes, it should," Ilana said.

"Why didn't the mist go through, then?"

Ilana's expression darkened. "It *is* that new barrier. You will have to be very creative if you want this to work."

Stefan arrived just then, the rest of their division trailing behind, and Amber took advantage of the momentary distraction to whisper, "Rain should go through. The mist would have counted as a large entity to that new barrier, so it did not get past. But rain will register as many small entities, small enough to pass through."

"Damn. How'd you come up with that?" Tristan asked

under his breath.

Amber reddened. "It wasn't supposed to be like that. It should have been a full weatherproof barrier. But I couldn't figure out how to do it."

"Well, good thing you couldn't." Again Tristan marveled at the irony—he was suddenly *grateful* for the weak barrier around the Lair, because he would do anything to bring it down. Without Drakewell and Natasha, who would believe them when they said they were trying to help the Lair? He was having a hard time believing it himself.

Once Stefan and the six other students were standing in a half-circle around the table, Ilana said, "Tristan and Amber are going to demonstrate a weakness in the enemy's dome. They will be flooding and burning down various buildings above the Lair, and all of this without being able to see the structures. Tristan, would you like to explain how you're planning to accomplish this?"

"There's a hole in the barrier," Tristan said. "Right where that mist is swirling." He pointed to the gap. "The botany longhouse is right under that, I think, and just a bit above it is the greenhouse. Then there's two empty longhouses to the right, and the third one is the entrance to the Lair. I'm—" He broke off, because he wasn't at all sure how he was meant to start a fire without seeing what he was burning. "I guess I'm going to reach that quill through the hole in the enchantment, and start the fire that way?"

He looked at Ilana for confirmation, and she gave him a sharp nod.

Stepping closer to the table, Tristan cleared his throat

and aimed the quill for the swirling patch of mist. He had to act quickly, because some of the mist was beginning to drift away. The jagged motion that summoned up a fire was all too familiar to him after their attack on Whitney the previous year, and with his nerves jangling, he channeled magic into the quill before he even tried.

Holding the quill between his thumb and forefinger, he made a careful zigzagging line that trailed from the Lair's entrance down over the next two buildings to finish at Gracewright's longhouse. When the quill collided with something above the table that he couldn't see, he knew with grim certainty that his spell had worked.

At last he lifted the conduit away, severing the flow of magic. The class waited in silence for several minutes; eventually a wisp of translucent smoke appeared in midair and began to drift up from the top of the dome. Three other columns of smoke joined it—his spell had worked. All four buildings were aflame.

And with all of the professors away, no one would be able to put out the fires.

He wondered darkly how many of them would guess he was involved after today. After all, he did have a rather bad streak of fires to his name.

"And now, Amber, are you ready to begin the flooding rains?"

"Uh…shouldn't we wait until the fires are done burning everything down?" Tristan asked. He had hoped to do this all himself, to save Amber from the crippling guilt he knew she would face.

Ilana frowned. "Your professors will notice very quickly that something is wrong. And if they realize we are behind the rains, they'll blow the clouds in the opposite direction. You know we don't have control over air magic, Tristan. We can't do anything against a stiff wind."

"Oh." Wishing the rest of the class would go away, Tristan handed the conduit to Amber, who took it with a blank expression. Remembering the way she had shut down completely after accidentally killing two magicians the previous year, he prayed that nothing unusual would happen this time around. If she overdid the spell and killed someone from the Lair, she might just snap.

Eyeing the dome, Amber lifted the glass quill and slowly began drawing forth a raincloud. A patch of the cloud hung low enough that it showed up as a new layer of fog lingering above the table, though the top was cut cleanly off where the globe's range ended. As the rain began to fall, the entire valley vanished beneath a haze of water. The rainstorm was trapped between the ring of mountains, which concentrated the deluge and prevented the clouds from blowing away.

"They'll know this was us," Ilana said with a cold smile. "They won't underestimate us again."

"But you're not worried they might guard against our earthquake?" Stefan asked.

"They can't," Ilana said. "I'm positive of it. There isn't any piece of magic in existence that can ward against earthquakes. You would have to construct a barrier through the earth itself to accomplish that."

Stefan grinned. "Beauty."

"It will be, won't it," Ilana said. "Now, how is this flooding going?"

Though it was hard to see through the curtain of rain, Tristan thought he could make out a river gushing off the side of one ridge. If enough water continued to fall, the entire meadow surrounding the Lair could be swamped. Whether or not the Lair itself was harmed, his friends might be unable to make it back through the entrance for several more days.

Amber's face remained carefully blank, yet Tristan thought she was doing her best to burn through Ilana's store of water magic. As he watched, the rain seemed to fall heavier still, the rain clouds expanding until even the peaks of the nearby mountains were trapped in the storm.

At last Ilana said, "That will be enough."

As if coming out of a trance, Amber blinked and lowered the conduit. The rain lessened enough for Tristan to see just how much the valley was flooding—waterfalls cascaded down every ridge and pooled in the valley, and the peaceful brook just west of the meadow had become a swollen torrent. Now that the storm was no longer fueled by magic, it would taper off on its own.

"Very well done," Ilana said, sounding impressed in spite of herself. "You could have been a bit more conservative with your use of magic, but perhaps it wouldn't have been so effective. Now, can someone tell me the volume of water that has accumulated in this valley?"

They spent the rest of the lesson calculating rough

volumes of rainwater based on the speed of rainfall and the estimated volume of the rivers that had formed off the hillsides. Tristan couldn't follow most of it; his main impression was that any breach in the Lair would be very badly flooded by now.

It was eight o'clock by the time Ilana released their division. On the way back up to their bedrooms, Rajesh fell into line beside Tristan and muttered, "You're not scared of killing everyone at your former school?" He looked a bit worried.

"No one's died today," Tristan whispered. "We just caused a bit of havoc."

Rajesh gave him a fleeting smile. "I think you've finally convinced Ilana. Well done." Almost immediately his smile was replaced by a brooding expression. "What'd you think of the seminar?"

"Does Ilana really believe all that stuff she was talking about? Because it almost made sense."

Rajesh snorted. "No way. Like I said, she's a psychopath." He dropped his voice further still. "Don't let Stefan hear you, though. He's in love with her. Half the teachers are."

When they reached their bedrooms, Amber drifted off to bed without a word. After his shower, Tristan knocked tentatively on her door and, when she didn't answer, pushed it softly open. He didn't want to disturb her if she was asleep.

But Amber sat hunched against the head of her bed, digging flakes of ice from the wall with her fingernail. She had already chipped away a hole the size of her fist.

"Are you okay?" Tristan asked, already knowing the answer.

"That rainstorm wasn't supposed to be so big," she whispered.

Tristan sat at the end of her bed and put a tentative hand on her knee. "Well, at least you burned through a ton of their marbles. I don't think Ilana can blame you for it, either."

She scratched at the wall more determinedly than ever. "I don't think they had time to repair that breach in the tunnels. The entire bottom half of the Lair could be flooded right now."

That was bad. Tristan tried to think of something reassuring to say, but he couldn't come up with anything short of lying. "Are you sure it's flooded?"

"I think so. They put a Prasidimum over the gap, but those don't guard against water. The entrance to the Lair will be fine, since it has a full barrier of some sort, but the rest will be a mess."

"Well, at least they were outside," Tristan said. "No one's been hurt."

Amber nodded slowly. "And Ilana trusts us now. How can we destroy her globe?"

Tristan glanced at the hole Amber was still chipping away at. "It's so well-fortified that we can't get in there alone. So we either have to dig through the walls or cause a diversion. I think we should try to map this place out. Then we'll know if it's even possible to dig through."

"Okay." Still Amber didn't meet Tristan's eyes. He wished he could have sent both disasters in her stead, to save her from such crushing regret. At least if he had messed up, he would have known he couldn't do any better. But Amber knew so much about magic that she felt fully responsible for anything she brought about.

Too wound-up to distract Amber from her misery, Tristan went to bed soon after that, wondering if he dared approach any of the other students about a map of the school.

But the right moment never came.

Chapter 7

Lost Magic

Five days after the flood, Tristan was harvesting water magic up on the ice sheet along with the rest of the First Division when the low hum of an engine sounded in the distance.

Stefan dropped his jar and jumped away from the stream, eyes on the overcast sky.

Seconds later, a small plane flew over the ice sheet, dropping lower as it approached the class.

"Go," Stefan said dazedly. "Run!"

Abandoning their jars and wheelbarrow beside the stream, the entire class took off in a dead run for the entrance to the school. Their strength training lessons had clearly paid off, because Tristan was hardly winded as he pounded across the ice close on Ricardo's heels.

It took ten minutes to reach the safety of the tunnels, and in that time the plane continued to circle, occasionally disappearing into the clouds for a moment before turning and dropping lower still. Tristan clutched a stitch in his side as he ran, glancing back at the plane whenever he dared. Just above the trapdoor, Stefan paused and said, "They'll see our entrance."

Blake grabbed the handle and yanked the trapdoor open. "They'll figure it out anyway." He jumped into the tunnel, not bothering with the ladder, and the others hastily followed. As soon as Tristan was safely inside, he dragged the trapdoor closed above him and locked the bolt.

Still running, Stefan took off for the globe room, the rest of the class following.

"Someone—get Ilana," he panted.

Mei Ling slowed and turned down an unfamiliar corridor; an instant later she was out of sight.

Inside the globe room, Stefan whirled the globe around to face Greenland. When he attached the disc to the right patch of ice, the seven remaining students clustered around the table.

"Can you see it?" Stefan asked.

Still breathing hard, Tristan scanned the sky for any sign of an airplane.

"Nothing, sir," Ricardo said.

Stefan cursed loudly. "They've found us. They've bloody well found us!"

"That wasn't the plane from the Lair," Tristan said. "Drakewell's plane doesn't have any company logo. That one said 'Air Zafari' or something on it."

Stefan's shoulders sagged in relief. "Then we may be lucky this time."

Ilana kicked open the door just then, a tiny red-headed

girl in her arms and Mei Ling close on her heels.

"What is this nonsense?" she snapped. "Mei Ling tells me you were *seen*. By a small airplane."

"We were," Stefan said darkly.

"And? How did you deal with the threat?"

"We hurried inside," Stefan said. "They looked as though they were about to land. I thought the plane might belong to the Lair."

"You idiot!" Ilana snarled.

The girl in her arms, who couldn't have been older than three, began to cry softly.

Ilana bounced the girl as she yelled, "Why didn't you throw a spell at the plane? You could have brought it down and saved us all from this mess. Anton's division wrecked *two* planes last year. His quick thinking kept any planes from flying in this area for fourteen months straight. But you've ruined everything."

"Maybe they just thought we were natives," Ricardo said.

Ilana gave him a look that said she was not in the mood for jokes. "Come with me, Division One. You will be reassigned."

Tristan didn't know what that meant, but Stefan blanched.

"Everyone must stay underground until I say otherwise," she continued. "If Rowan Drakewell is half as intelligent as I remember, he will hear about this."

"Do we have a barrier up around this school?" Tristan asked Stefan as Ilana hurried the class back up the corridor.

"No," he said grimly. "And your magician friends are about to figure that out. We aren't safe here."

"Could we put something up?"

Stefan shook his head. "The barrier at your school was erected hundreds of years ago. No one remembers how."

At a cold look from Ilana, he stopped talking. For the first time, Tristan realized how young Stefan was—no older than twenty-five. He looked very much like a reprimanded student as he followed Ilana down the tunnel to the cafeteria.

Though it was still mid-morning, two other divisions had already assembled in the cafeteria, sitting in silence as they awaited instruction. Ilana left Tristan's division there and led Stefan away, her face lined with anger.

Tristan didn't see Stefan again for weeks.

The rest of the school had assembled by the time Ilana returned, the red-headed girl no longer in her arms.

One of the teachers—a short, curly-haired woman— had a laptop open at the teachers' table, and several other teachers were looking over her shoulder, breaking the usual air of tight discipline that prevailed in the cafeteria.

"Nothing yet," the short woman said. "Wait—there. 'Colony of eccentrics spotted on Greenland ice sheet.'"

Ilana pulled a chair up beside the woman and yanked the laptop closer. "Read it, Amelia."

The curly-haired woman cleared her throat. "On a routine flightseeing tour up to Tasiilaq, Air Zafari captain Henrik Rasmussen spotted a group of nine people on the ice cap. The group fled as the plane approached, disappearing underground through a hole in the ice. The group was not dressed in traditional Inuit garb, and is therefore suspected to be part of an off-grid settlement recently suspected of taking up residence on the ice cap. There are no legal records of a non-native population establishing itself on the ice cap, and further investigations will take place to confirm the sighting."

"There's even a photo," Ilana said through her teeth. "A *photo*. Stefan is a complete imbecile. He's ruined everything." She turned the laptop to show the rest of the students, most of whom had abandoned their usual seats and clustered around the teachers' table. Sure enough, there was a blurry snapshot of the ice sheet with nine figures sprinting toward the edge of the frame. Beside Tristan, Ricardo groaned. Tristan's spine tingled with excitement. Did this mean Drakewell had found them? Was the Lair going to step in and help?

"We can just stay underground, though, can't we?" Blake asked, huge hands fisted on the table in front of him. "The media will get bored if they don't see anything else."

"It's not the *media* we're worried about, idiot boy. It's Rowan Drakewell. He'll know exactly what that report means. And we don't have any barrier whatsoever around this place. We've lost that knowledge." She looked sharply at Amber. "How did your school put up a new barrier? Who figured it out?"

Amber dropped her eyes, looking terrified. "W-we did it together. The entire school channeled their power into the f-frame. But we used the magic of the forest to feed the barrier. It would not work here."

Ilana swore. "Rowan is trying to flush us out of our hole. And he's succeeded. He really has. We can't stay here and wait to be attacked. It would put us in the same situation your school was in last year. The only question is, where can we go?"

Every eye was locked on Ilana now. Tristan realized with a start that some of these students had been living in Ilana's ice cave since they were babies; their only knowledge of the outside world lay in their experiences with the globe. And setting foot on foreign soils was very different from sending disasters at the roughly-hewn countries on the globe. He could only imagine what a shock that would be.

"Couldn't we just hide in a city?" he asked before he could stop himself. "No one would be able to find us with so many auras around."

"We can't harvest magic in a city," Ilana snapped. "You should know that by now."

Tristan flushed.

"Any other suggestions? Tristan, Amber, we're counting on you. Where is the place your professors would least expect to find us? We could always head back to Canada, but I have a feeling they will be watching that region very closely."

He had no idea. "Somewhere in the southern hemisphere, probably," he said slowly. "They haven't even finished fixing their maps for most of those countries. You should thank Merridy—she's the one who wrecked those tables in the first place." He felt a sudden pang as he remembered that Alldusk still didn't know Merridy was dead.

When Ilana's eyes widened in triumph, he immediately regretted his words. He had just ensured, once and for all, that he and Amber were cut off entirely from the Lair.

No one would be helping them now. This task was theirs alone.

"So. Where will it be? Not Antarctica, because we run the risk of exposing ourselves like we did here. We have to go somewhere with more people to lose ourselves among, and enough magic to weave our own barrier." Ilana gave Amber a sharp look. "I expect your help with this, missy."

Amber swallowed.

A slightly chubby teacher spoke up. "We could always go to New Zealand," he said hopefully. His nasal accent gave him away as a Kiwi.

"You don't regret joining me, do you, Tony?" Ilana asked coldly. "You're not seeking a way to escape my service?"

"'Course not. But there *are* lots of caves in New Zealand. Unexplored ones, too."

Amber glanced sideways at Tristan. For the first time in a week, the faintest smile tugged at her lips.

She was probably starved for magic here. Anywhere but this godforsaken ice sheet would feel like heaven to her.

"I'll consider your idea," Ilana said. "We will spend the next four days preparing for our departure, including digging the globe out of its chamber. In the meantime, I would love to hear any further suggestions of where we ought to reestablish ourselves. Tony, you can take over the First Division while Stefan is incapacitated."

"Good as gold," Tony said.

"All lessons will be suspended," Ilana said. "Return to your rooms and pack your belongings. I want to see all of you back here in one hour."

Just as Tristan was turning to follow Rajesh from the cafeteria, Ilana grabbed Amber's wrist.

"Not you," she said. "I need to speak with you."

"Can I come too?" Tristan asked, worried.

A gust of air pummeled Tristan so hard in the gut that he fell backwards and collided with a table.

"Don't be so presumptuous," Ilana hissed, while Tristan struggled to right himself. "Get back to your room this instant, or you'll regret ever coming here."

With a desperate look at Amber, whose face was stony, Tristan turned and slunk from the cafeteria.

"What was that about?" Rajesh muttered. He'd been waiting in the doorway.

"Ilana wants to talk to Amber."

"Uh-oh. That's never good."

Tristan grimaced. "I hope Amber doesn't do anything rash…"

"Doesn't matter what she does if Ilana's not happy with her. She doesn't need an excuse to beat us up."

Tristan stopped in his tracks. "I should go after her—"

"No," Rajesh said firmly. "That'll only make it worse." They were the last ones in the hallway, so Rajesh lowered his voice and said, "Do you actually think it's your school that found us?"

"Yeah. I didn't think they would look for us, but..." He had a fleeting image of Leila sitting beside the globe with the lights off, searching fruitlessly for a set of bright auras she thought she might never find.

Rajesh gave Tristan a reassuring pat on the shoulder when they parted ways. "I think she's stronger than she looks. She'll be okay."

Tristan nodded without conviction. He had nothing to pack in his bedroom, so he just sat on his bed, its end heaped with untidy blankets, and stared at the icy walls. What had Amber done wrong? Did Ilana suspect her of helping the Lair in some way—of giving away their location?

He flopped back on his pillows, grinding the heels of his palms into his eyes. What had Drakewell hoped to accomplish by exposing the ice cave? Did he intend to attack Ilana directly, or did he believe Tristan and Amber would have an easier time destroying the globe while it was being relocated?

If the latter was the case, Drakewell had more confidence in their abilities than Tristan did. They had no access to marbles, and he still couldn't perform any sort of magic without them, aside from the time he had done it on accident to stop Merridy from killing everyone at the Lair. Amber was equally powerless without any living nature to draw from, though she might have more luck if they did relocate to New Zealand rather than some barren desert in Africa or Australia.

Lying on his bed, Tristan tried to summon up a spell to warm himself, the easiest magic he could think of. He concentrated so fiercely that his head began to ache, but nothing happened. At last he gave up, throwing his pillow onto the floor in frustration. This cave just felt so dead, so devoid of magic, that he might as well have tried to wring water from a rock.

Unwilling to face what lay ahead, Tristan turned his thoughts to his friends at the Lair. Were Eli, Trey, Hayley, and Cailyn still playing poker with their pile of gold discs? Did Evvie miss him at all, or did she resent him for ruining their only date? And had Zeke asked Leila out yet? This last thought had him seething with anger. Zeke didn't deserve Leila. He was a good-for-nothing prick, and if Leila ever agreed to go out with him, she would only get hurt.

But he was dead in Leila's eyes. He had no right to judge her or deny her whatever happiness she could find.

As much as he hoped to distract himself with thoughts of the Lair, he couldn't stop thinking about Amber.

Was she hurt?

Was she…

He forced away the terrible thought. Angrier than before, he jumped to his feet and began pacing the tiny room, kicking his pillow every time he stumbled over it.

The end of the hour came sooner than he expected; when someone rapped at his door, he slammed the pillow back onto his messy bed and dragged his hair into place over his scars. "I'm coming," he yelled when the knock sounded again. Yanking open the door, he almost tripped over the same tiny Scandinavian girl who had first summoned him to classes. "Sorry," he said, trying to reel in his temper.

The girl did not reply. Turning with precision, she strode down the hall, stopping to knock at each subsequent door.

In the cafeteria, the students were whispering among themselves, looking more alive than Tristan had ever seen them. Blake and Ricardo kept shooting furtive looks at Tony, while Rajesh was saying something in an undertone to Mei Ling, who was stoically ignoring him.

As soon as Ilana returned, smiling dangerously, the conversation died immediately while every student scrambled to resume their seats.

Amber had not returned.

Tristan wanted to confront Ilana on the spot and demand that she release Amber, but he would gain nothing by making an enemy of her. His position was too uncertain as it was.

"As I said earlier, we will be leaving this place behind in four days," Ilana said, standing behind her usual chair with a hand on the Irish pilot's shoulder. "We will split into fifteen groups, five students with each teacher, and every group will take a different route to reach our new base. Unless anyone comes to me with a different idea, we will take Tony's advice and relocate to New Zealand."

Tony's eyes widened in triumph.

"I will read out your assigned groups today, and over the next two days Anton and I will arrange transportation to your new home." She squeezed the pilot's shoulder. "We will book flights with multiple airlines, each taking a different route to our destination and each arriving at a separate time. I will personally transport our globe on a fishing boat that Mordechai has procured for us, with two of your teachers accompanying me. The globe will not arrive for several months, and I expect your new home to be fit for human habitation by the time I join you."

She looked sharply around the teachers' table at this, waiting until every teacher nodded or said, "Yes, Ilana."

"In the meantime, you'll be harvesting magic more intensively than ever. We need to act quickly or risk being discovered a second time. How long until the Lair's southern hemisphere is reconstructed, Tristan?"

Tristan straightened abruptly, caught off guard. "Um…at least a year, I think."

"Good. We needed two years to carry out our original plan, but with your help and Amber's, I believe we can speed up the process a bit."

Tristan relaxed marginally. Wherever Amber was, at least Ilana planned to keep her alive.

Raising her voice, Ilana said, "Mordechai!"

The cafeteria doors ground open once more to admit the fierce-looking tattooed man who had threatened Tristan. He was dragging a wagon loaded to the brim with blue, gold, and green marbles.

"Division Five, please stand and form a line behind Mordechai." Thirteen students from the end of Tristan's table pushed back their benches and stood, eyeing

Mordechai with trepidation. "One at a time, please take ten marbles of each element. These will be yours to safeguard for the duration of your journey. Your teachers will reclaim the marbles when we reach our new home, and you'll be held accountable for any that are found missing."

From her tone, Tristan guessed she would not stop at torturing any students who lost a piece of her precious magic hoard.

Once Division Five was finished, Ilana proceeded through the remaining divisions. A sizable stack of marbles remained in the cart by the time Tristan's division had taken their share, almost half of the original pool, but Ilana did not divide the marbles further. She waved Mordechai out of the cafeteria and took her seat at last.

"Understand this, my precious children," Ilana said, hands clasped in front of her as she addressed the students. "You will be faced with choices and dangers that you've never seen before once you leave the protection of my school. If word of your powers were to reach mortal ears, you would be hated and feared and locked away. Guard your secrets carefully, my children, and prove to me that I have chosen well in my disciples."

Mortal ears? That couldn't be right. Tristan frowned at Ilana, unsure what she meant by it. Magicians were no less mortal than anyone else. Had she seduced her followers with promises of immortality? Or had she tricked them into believing themselves *gods?*

They were divided up after that—Tristan would be traveling under Tony's guard, along with Rajesh and Mei

Ling; a scrawny, angry-looking boy Tristan had never seen before who appeared from outside the cafeteria when summoned; and a black girl who could have been no older than five. Tony tickled the little girl when she joined them, and her solemn expression dissolved into helpless giggles.

When Ilana gave Tony a stern look, he shrugged and put on a mock-repentant frown.

"Back to your rooms, all of you," Ilana said once the students were divided between the teachers. She hadn't assigned Amber to a group.

One day before they began to flee, Ilana made her final decision—they would relocate to the Bulmer cave system on the South Island of New Zealand, which was occasionally visited by tourists but remained for the most part unexplored. Tony hardly attempted to hide his glee.

The flights were booked, the groups staggered across a week of departures. Tristan's group would be one of the first to leave—he suspected Ilana wanted him out of the way—and they were flying Virgin Australia through London, Dubai, and Sydney. He had never flown such a long way before; indeed, he had never owned a passport.

That evening, Anton came around the cafeteria handing out passports to each of the students. They must have accessed some sort of online records, because Tristan's passport had the same photo that had been on his driver's permit, with the correct date of birth. The passports circulating through the room were multicolored—red British passports went to most of the younger students, while the older students and teachers were matched with their countries of birth. Rajesh got a blue Indian passport, Mei Ling a rust-colored Chinese passport, and Ori's was Israeli. Well, that solved one mystery.

On his way back to his room, Tristan flipped through the passport, noticing that it had a Greenland stamp on the first page dated one month prior. He was so absorbed that he nearly ran into Amber, who stood in the hallway looking halfway dead.

Tristan's heart leapt. "Amber! My god, where have you been?"

Her eyes were hollow, her hair lanky and unkempt. When Tristan drew her into a hug, she flinched and tried to pull away from him.

He released her quickly. "Are you hurt?"

She hung her head and said nothing.

Taking her hand, Tristan pulled Amber into his room and said urgently, "What the hell did she do to you? Why did she take you away?"

Amber shook her head. After a long silence, she whispered, "Ilana knew. She knew I used air magic to direct that mist. She—she forced me to gather a hundred silver marbles for her hoard."

Tristan cursed. Amber would not have agreed to harvest air magic easily; she had never revealed her secrets to Delair, and it would have killed her to give Ilana such an edge.

"They *tortured* you." Tristan was horrified.

Amber's silence was answer enough.

"Let me see." Cautiously, Tristan reached out and rolled up Amber's sleeve past the elbow. She held herself stiffly, which meant it hurt more than she wanted to admit.

Bruises mottled the length of her arm, purple and yellow, and a barely-healed cut ran from her elbow down the inside of her arm to her wrist.

"Who did this?" Tristan spat. "*Who?*"

Swallowing, Amber pulled her arm away and turned down her sleeve again. "No one."

"Come on, Amber. I'm gonna kill whoever did that to you."

"That's why I can't say," she whispered. "It will ruin all of our plans."

"Screw them. Screw Drakewell! We have to leave."

"No." Amber sat on the bed, flinching again, and folded her hands in her lap. "There's a reason Ilana needed exactly a hundred air marbles. She found the records of an ancient spell that will eventually cause more damage alone than two years' worth of disasters on the globe. And now she has every piece she needs for it. A globe, and a hundred marbles of each element."

"And she didn't mind telling you about it?"

Amber shook her head. "She'll enact the spell on her way to New Zealand. The globe and the marbles will travel with her, and we will be thousands of miles away, helpless to stop her."

Tristan grabbed the door-handle. "We have to warn Drakewell."

"No. We don't have any way to contact him. We have to destroy that globe. It's the only hope we have."

Chapter 8

Beyond the Map

To Tristan's immense relief, Amber was assigned to his group the following morning. Her empty, hopeless expression lingered; he was worried she would do something rash if she was pushed too far again.

"You okay?" he whispered when he saw her at breakfast.

She met his eyes but said nothing.

He grew restless as the morning passed, desperate to do something that would stop Ilana from enacting whatever horrible spell she had planned, yet unable to think of anything he *could* do. He could try to run for it, but he wouldn't make it far. And there was no way for him to evade the watchful eyes of the teachers long enough to do anything on his own.

Two hours before Tristan's group was scheduled to leave, Tony came barreling into the cafeteria, shouting, "They've sent a bloody ice-storm! Anton's just flown off to keep the plane safe, but he'll be back when it stops. They're using our own idea against us, the bastards!"

Ilana did not look surprised. "It's a warning," she said. "We were right to leave."

Tristan took grim pleasure in the knowledge that Drakewell had discovered their location. Although they were about to abandon this frozen rabbit-warren, he found comfort in the fact that Drakewell was in the Map Room at this very moment, keeping an eye on Greenland. It made him feel just a fraction less isolated.

It was funny—a few years back, he would have given anything to visit New Zealand. One of his wealthy classmates had gone in seventh grade, and returned with grand stories of seeing Middle-Earth in real life. Now, he hated the thought of going any farther from the Lair.

"Fetch your bags," Ilana said. "Tony, wait with your group below the trapdoor until Anton announces the all-clear."

Tristan followed Rajesh and Mei Ling back to their bedrooms, where he grabbed the small backpack Ilana had given him, packed with thirty marbles and enough clothes to convince the airport security that he would be vacationing in New Zealand. Then he joined Tony—who was holding the little girl, Emma—at the foot of the ladder. Amber fell into place beside him a moment later, stony-faced, and Rajesh and Mei Ling arrived not long after. The scrawny, fierce-looking kid—Landen, whom Tristan was still convinced he had never seen before the night the students had been divided up—showed up last of all, with a duffel bag slung over one shoulder.

Anton flipped open the trapdoor before long, mopping sweat from his neck with a handkerchief.

"Bloody close call, that was," he said. "Hurry along. I wouldn't be surprised if that school sent another storm as soon as it caught sight of our auras."

Tristan doubted it. Whatever Drakewell's motives, he would not have gone to such great lengths just to risk killing Tristan and Amber in a storm.

As soon as they had settled into Anton's plane, Tony relaxed.

"C'mere, munchkin," he said, holding out his arms for Emma. She jumped into his lap and consented to be buckled into place, though a moment later she bounced up on the seat, tucked her legs under her, and tried to look out the window. Only then did Tristan realize he had never heard her speak a word. It seemed that Ilana had managed to instill a fearful brand of discipline even in her youngest students.

Tristan couldn't help but stare out the window as well once they had taken off. They rose over the vast, rippling ice cap before cutting south, the mountains growing taller and rockier as they went. Not a creature stirred on the ice below, save a pair of hairy animals that looked like misplaced wooly mammoths. Once the plane had leveled out above a layer of wispy clouds, Tony stood and dug in a bag at his feet.

"You'll have to change," he said, tossing a set of clothes at Tristan. "Tristan, Rajesh, and Landen, you're flying to the semifinals for the junior rugby cup. Emma and

Mei Ling, you're with me. I have your adoption papers. And Amber, you're on your own. Visiting relatives for a holiday. Try not to cause any trouble."

Unfolding the pile of clothes, Tristan found jeans, a rugby team sweatshirt, and a beat-up pair of sneakers. Rajesh and Landen had the same, though Rajesh's sneakers were blindingly white. Tristan didn't like the idea of traveling with Landen, but he supposed Ilana wanted someone keeping an eye on him. There had to be a reason he wasn't part of one of the regular divisions.

They changed on the plane, carefully avoiding one another's eyes. Emma got to keep her fur boots and fur-lined parka, but Amber was given a pair of slim black pants and a dress shirt that made her look much older than seventeen, while Mei Ling had to wear an awful bejeweled Minnie Mouse t-shirt that she glared at before pulling it over her tank top.

As they settled back into their seats, all eyeing one another's new clothes, Emma tugged Tony's sleeve and whispered loudly, "Can you braid my hair again? Like that other time?"

"Sure thing, sweetie."

Emma's hair had been straightened, and it came easily into two French braids under Tony's expert fingers. Clearly he had done this more than once.

Before long they were descending past mountains towards a harbor lined with colorful houses. On the runway, Tristan ran to catch up with Amber. "Are you *sure* you're okay?"

This time she nodded. "I will be."

It had to be enough. They were at the airport doors now, and Anton waved them off from the cockpit of his tiny plane.

In groups, they approached the ticketing counter and presented their passports. Tristan's heart thudded as he waited for the ticketing agent to check his, but he needn't have worried—seconds later, he was handed four boarding passes and pointed toward the bag drop.

"Not much security here," Rajesh said in an undertone. "It'd be a lot different if any of us were trying to get into the U.S. Except for you and Amber, of course."

Tristan nodded distractedly. On the first flight, he sat by himself near the rear of the plane, and he was very relieved to find Rajesh and Landen waiting for him just outside the gate at Heathrow. He, Rajesh, and Landen had middle-row seats together on this flight aboard a Boeing 747, the largest airplane Tristan had ever set foot in.

As soon as the seatbelt sign turned off, Landen was prowling the aisle, returning half an hour later to eat dinner. Then he was off again.

When he vanished for the second time, Tristan gathered his courage and asked Rajesh, "Would you—fight against Ilana? If you could?"

Rajesh raised an eyebrow. "That's dangerous talk."

Tristan waited.

"I would, though. You keep your mouth shut, because I'm dead if she finds out. But yes, I hate it there. I'd do anything to stop Ilana before—"

"Good," Tristan said softly. "Because I'm going to need your help." Glancing furtively down the aisle in search of Landen's return, he explained everything—Drakewell's orders that he and Amber had to destroy Ilana's globe before it was too late; the way Ilana had tortured Amber for a hundred silver marbles; and her plans to enact a spell more powerful than anything the globe alone could accomplish. Rajesh listened, wide-eyed, and did not speak for a long time after Tristan had finished.

Tristan knew he was taking a major gamble in giving himself away, but with Ilana far behind for the time being, he would never get a better chance to speak openly. And his time was growing short.

"I bet Ilana's planning to enact that spell while she's on that boat," Rajesh said at last, picking apart the lamination on his flight safety card. "She knows she's made an enemy of Amber, so this spell must be worth the risk. She's actually scared of you guys, did you know that?"

Tristan snorted. "I'm useless. It's Amber who could probably kill us all with a look if she wanted to. Why don't you support Ilana, anyway? I thought most of the students at your school were brainwashed."

"Some of them are. Especially the younger ones." Rajesh glanced over Tristan's head, also on the lookout for Landen. "But everyone my age, we were five years old when we started with Ilana. It doesn't sound like much, but it was enough to figure some things out."

"What happened?"

Rajesh shoved his flight card back into the mesh

pocket. "My baby sister died. Ilana took both of us in, pretended she was doing us a kindness. Fatima was only seven months old when we arrived in Greenland, and she was always a bit sickly. I don't think she ever got cared for properly. They're better now, but back then…"

Clearing his throat, Rajesh continued. "When she was four, she got sick. Really sick. She had an awful fever, and she was crying all the time. I begged Ilana to take her to a hospital, but she locked me in my room and refused. By the time I was let out, Fatima was dead and everyone had forgotten about her."

"I'm really sorry," Tristan said, his voice shaking. "My little brother is dead, too. It was Drakewell's fault—he set the whole thing up when he wanted to recruit me—but it was my hand on the steering wheel when the car crashed."

Rajesh gripped Tristan's arm and met his eyes at last. There was fear behind his gaze, and unfathomable pain. "Don't let it destroy you, okay? I nearly did. I almost gave up afterwards. I can hardly remember anything from that time. Then we sent a disaster to India, right near where I came from, and I snapped out of it all at once. Now I've just been waiting for the right chance. Ilana can't hurt me any more than she already has. Whatever you have to do, I'll help you with it."

"Thank you." Tristan swallowed against the lump in his throat.

As he settled back into his seat, he realized that, for the first time in his life, he had spoken the words that he had long denied himself—*it was Drakewell's fault*. Yes, Tristan had made a rash, idiotic decision on that fateful night, but it was Drakewell who had sent the earthquake, Drakewell who had lit the fire in his father's home, and Drakewell who had ensured the key sat ready in his neighbor's car.

With that thought, the heavy weight that had suffocated Tristan for two years finally eased its grip.

He was not a murderer, just stupid beyond belief.

And dwelling on the car crash would solve nothing. He had to ensure that no one else died senselessly, to stop Ilana before she sent any more innocent people following in Marcus's footsteps. He would honor Marcus's memory by doing the right thing now.

Just then, a commotion in the aisle sent passengers turning in their seats and unbuckling their seatbelts to look for the source of the scuffle.

Tristan didn't have to wait long for the mystery to resolve itself. Tony staggered to their row, dragging a limp, scowling Landen by one arm.

"You're going to *sit still* until the end of the flight, mate," Tony said. "Rajesh and Tristan'll make sure you do."

Landen dropped into his seat without a word and clicked his buckle emphatically into place. "I'm sure they will," he said sourly.

When Tony had returned to his seat, shaking his head, Tristan gave Landen a curious sideways look. "Why aren't you in any of the divisions?"

"Mind your own business," Landen snapped.

"He's with Mordechai," Rajesh said. "He gets all the kids who won't behave. Blake used to be one of them, and look at him now."

Landen looked as though he wanted to strangle Rajesh, though eventually he dug up a pair of headphones and began watching *The Dark Knight*, gripping the armrests with his bony fingers.

Hours passed. Tristan dozed fitfully, coming awake every time his head dropped onto his shoulder, his dreams filled with scenes of the Lair. Marcus was in one of them, throwing snowballs at Zeke and Damian, and Amber stood behind him, whispering in his ear that they ought to just run away...

At the Dubai airport, Tristan wished Tony was there to supervise them through customs. Of course, Amber would be going through the airport entirely on her own, so he didn't really have anything to complain about. Landen followed two steps behind Tristan and Rajesh through the sprawling airport terminal, and when they stopped at the toilets, he took ages to reappear. When he still hadn't emerged after twenty minutes, Tristan and Rajesh bent over to check under every stall, but they didn't recognize Landen's shoes in any of them.

"What're we supposed to do?" Tristan asked in exasperation, shoving open the bathroom door for the second time.

"He's not our problem," Rajesh said grimly. "We should head to the gate and tell Tony what's happened."

Tristan didn't need any more persuasion. They shouldered their backpacks and continued down the wide hall toward their third flight. "Why does Ilana put up with kids like that?"

"If she breaks them right, they'll be her most devoted followers." Rajesh looked as though he had eaten a lemon. "Blake was one of them, and now he's as ruthless as she is. She'd probably marry him if she could."

It was hard to imagine that Blake, blond and built like a football star, had once been as much trouble as Landen. Now he seemed the image of sophisticated strength.

When Tony saw Tristan and Rajesh heading his way, he shook his head vigorously to warn them away. They went up to him anyway, and Rajesh broke the news.

"Landen's vanished. Last we saw, he was in a bathroom back that way."

"That little bastard! Emma, can you wait here with Mei Ling? I'll be back in a sec."

Tristan and Rajesh chose seats on the opposite side of the gate. Another half-hour passed before Tony reappeared, Landen marching along before him and kicking everything he passed.

"If you do that again, you're not eating anything for a week." Tony gave Landen a push in the direction of the gate, where he flopped into the seat beside Tristan.

"I hate him." Landen threw his duffle bag at the seat opposite him, nearly whacking an old man on the shoulder.

"He's got to be better than Mordechai, though," Rajesh said.

"I hate him too."

As they waited for their flight, Tristan eyed the gift

shop, wondering if he could send a postcard warning of Ilana's scheme to Millersville in the vague hope that someone from the Lair might stumble across it. But he didn't have any money, and when he made a circuit of the gift shop just to see if he could steal a postcard without being caught, he was dismayed to see that all of the stamps were hanging safely behind the counter.

Hopelessness plagued him as he returned to his seat. Ilana was thousands of miles away now, and there was nothing he could do to stop her.

Many hours later, eyes aching and head pounding, Tristan stumbled off their final short flight from Auckland to Nelson. He was too tired to appreciate much aside from the fact that they were finally, blessedly, outside again; with a drizzling fog hiding most of their surroundings, he could only make out snatches of coastline and sections of pine trees growing in such unnaturally straight rows that they must have been planted. Everything smelled so fresh and alive after hours of breathing stale air.

They drove away from the airport in a white tour van on the wrong side of the road, Emma sleeping with her head on Mei Ling's lap and Landen snoring softly in the far back. They stopped once for supplies and a toilet break, and Tony didn't return for several hours. Briefly Tristan considered running for it—this might be his last chance— but instead he fell asleep.

The van now piled with food and camping supplies, they drove on, the road growing narrower with each turn and finally giving way to gravel. At the end of the road, Tony stood and stretched but didn't give any instructions. A while later, he opened the side door and said, "Rise and shine." He had set up a pair of tents in the trees not far from the gravel parking lot, beside a picnic table and an outhouse. "We've got a bit of a tramp tomorrow, so rest up."

Tristan stumbled into the closest tent and crawled into one of the down sleeping bags waiting inside. He was asleep before the tent door was zipped shut.

He woke in darkness, with someone's arm splayed across his shoulder and someone else's elbow digging into his ribs. When he went outside to relieve himself, the clouds had lifted to reveal a stunning canvas of stars. It was icy out; he wished he hadn't left his parka behind.

Before long the others began to stir, and the sun rose reluctantly in a peach sky.

"Who's going to pack away the tents?" Tony asked. "And we'll need to fit everything in these." He threw a set of five backpacks onto the gravel behind the van.

"Where's mine?" Emma asked, wide-eyed.

"You can use this." He dug in the van and handed her the small backpack Tristan had used for the flight over.

Thirty minutes later, all of their supplies had somehow been shoved into the five backpacks, and with dubious looks, the students tried lifting them for the first time. Tristan could barely get his off the ground, filled as it was with about fifty cans of food and a camping stove. He had to sit on the trunk and buckle himself in before he stood, back and shoulders protesting.

"All good?" Tony asked.

Tristan and Rajesh groaned. As they started off across a swing bridge, Tristan fell to the rear of the group, Amber just in front of him. Her eyes were still glazed over, whether with exhaustion or pain he could not tell, but he did not dare ask her what was wrong. He didn't want to call attention to her in front of the others.

They hiked up a long ridge and down a rocky chute into a valley still dappled with snow—after a moment of confusion, Tristan remembered that the seasons were switched down here, so what should have been a fine spring day in May was nearly winter in New Zealand. Landen must have taken Tony's threat seriously, because he trailed directly behind the teacher without hesitation.

After hours of hiking, Tristan's knees and back ached so much he wasn't sure he could continue much farther. He was just about to beg for a water break when they came to a small hut in the middle of a snowy valley.

"What's that doing there?" Rajesh asked.

"It's just a backcountry hut," Tony said. "The second group's going to join us here, and we'll head to the cave tomorrow morning." He looked happier than Tristan had ever seen him. "And after that, we're going deep into the wilderness. No one will ever find us here."

Chapter 9

Earth Magic

L ate that evening, the second group joined theirs. Headed by the curly-haired teacher, Amelia, it consisted of Blake, Ricardo, and a pair of identical twin girls no older than twelve who looked as though they came from somewhere in South America.

The following morning, they donned as many layers as they could find and started up the valley. After passing carefully over a set of marble bluffs riddled with treacherous crevasses half-hidden beneath the snow, they descended to a grassy shelf with an opening into the Bulmer cave system. Tristan's back hurt more with each step, the heavy cans threatening to crush him, but aside from his knees, his legs were hardly sore. Evidently their strength training was paying off at last.

"There won't be any tourists this time of year," Tony said. "It's a good time to get set up." He dropped his pack with a loud clank of cans and tossed around a set of headlamps. "Be really careful. I don't want to explain why we're a few students short when Ilana gets here."

Blake laughed. Dropping his pack at the back of the group, Tristan scrutinized him, wondering how he could possibly have been as bad as Landen.

"There's a big chamber off to the right, I think. Follow me."

Abandoning his supplies, Tony ducked into the cave and switched on his headlamp. The others fell into line behind him, Tristan and Amber taking up the rear. As he picked his way over rubble and uneven ground, Tristan kept tripping and catching himself on the wall. The pale beam of his headlamp was woefully inadequate in such a vast cavern.

Down a short slope, the cavern narrowed to a tunnel, finally forcing everyone but Emma to drop onto their hands and knees and crawl through the final stretch. On the other side, the cave widened again to form a wide, almost flat chamber ringed with stalactites and stalagmites.

"We'll stay in here," Tony said. "There's a lot more to explore, but we'll play it safe for now. Grab your bags, and we'll see if we can make this place a bit cozier.

As they began unpacking their supplies, stacking food in one corner and spreading mats and sleeping bags along the far wall, Tristan felt a wave of homesickness for the Lair. How excited he and his friends had been when they first discovered the Subroom—it had been a refuge, a place to call their own, and it had brought them together as never before.

A small part of him wished he could recreate that here,

with Amber and Rajesh and anyone who chose to support them, but he quickly discarded the idea. If he started treating Ilana's followers like friends, he might have a hard time remembering why he'd come here in the first place.

Once their supplies were more or less organized and most of the sleeping mats had been unrolled, Blake and Ricardo vanished down a new tunnel to explore the depths of the cave.

Glancing at Amber, Tristan asked Tony if they were allowed to explore outside.

"Don't go running off," he said.

"If I was planning to do that, I would've left at one of the airports," Tristan said. "You couldn't do much if we decided to leave anyway. I guess you'll just have to trust us."

"Very funny," Tony said drily, though he let them go.

They switched off their headlamps as soon as they could see the pale light streaming in from the cave mouth, and when they stepped into the sunlight, Amber tilted her face to the sky.

"I feel like I'm alive again," she said weakly. "Let's go for a walk, shall we?"

Tristan agreed at once, mostly because he wanted to talk to her where there was no chance of being overheard. The grassy flat was riddled with stones, and scrawny bushes poked from the snow here and there. As they circled around the hill, leaving the cave behind, Amber lifted her arms and breathed deeply. Tristan almost thought he could see her aura returning, a glow that strengthened as they moved.

"You're okay now?" he asked with a smile as she stopped to perch on a rocky outcropping.

"I think so." There was more life in her eyes than he had seen in weeks.

"And your arms?"

From the way she winced when he sat beside her, he realized it was more than just her arms that Ilana had damaged. After a long pause, she rolled up her left sleeve to show that the bruises were beginning to fade, the long gash turning to a scar.

"Ilana can't hurt me here," she said bravely. "I have all of this to draw on." She spread her arms wide as though to embrace the mountains and forest below. "She thinks she's taken us away from Drakewell's protection, but she's actually just given me back my powers."

Tristan was so relieved that he drew Amber into a fierce hug. She flinched but eventually relaxed into his embrace, arms tentatively slipping around his waist.

"I was so damn worried about you," Tristan whispered. "I could barely sleep all week. If Ilana was here right now, I'd kill her. I swear I would."

Amber shivered in his arms. "I hate her. She would do anything for revenge."

"Do you think that's what this is all about? Revenge?"

Amber shrugged. "I have a hard time understanding most people, but Ilana I don't understand at all." She disentangled herself from Tristan's arms and looked pensively back at the cave. "We only have two months before Ilana arrives. And she will have more than enough time to work her spell before then. The whole way to New Zealand, I was trying to think of some way to stop her, but I don't think we can. We just have to destroy the globe as soon as we see it again."

"Definitely," Tristan said. "And I couldn't think of anything either. Rajesh will help us, by the way. And I bet some of the others would, too."

"That would be too dangerous!" Amber said. "If anyone reports us, we're finished."

"We'll have to be careful, then. I don't think they're all bad. Rajesh can probably help us figure out who we can trust." Tristan hesitated. "How are we supposed to finish off the globe? Ilana's not stupid. She'll know if something is up."

"I'm not sure." Amber dug her toe into a snowdrift. "Let me think about it. If we had a barrier, and a few hundred marbles rigged to explode…"

Over the next two weeks, students and teachers continued to arrive. They brought news in waves—Ilana, Anton, and a teacher named Cody had started their voyage; storms continued to wrack the Greenland ice cap, enough that they made headlines; and Stefan would be flying down with the last group, which apparently meant he had been forgiven.

Life here was rougher than Tristan had expected. At least they no longer had to worry about cleaning toilets, because they didn't even have a toilet to clean. It was a week before one of the teachers brought back a composting toilet and installed it near the cave entrance, and not much longer before it began to reek.

To his surprise, Tristan liked it much better than living in Ilana's ice-cave. Mostly he enjoyed being away from her all-knowing glare, but he also liked the comfort of being surrounded once more by living nature.

"It's amazing," Amber told Tristan one night, lying back on her pallet and looking up at the glowworms that dotted the ceiling. "I feel as though I can see properly again after months of living in the dark. Everything here is so *alive*. It's incredible. Even the cave! Look, the rock is full of magic. It's alive, not like the Lair. And those glowworms!"

Tristan laughed. "Maybe we'd be better off just staying here."

"Funny," Amber said.

The students had let their guard down in Ilana's absence, and dinners that had once been held in silence were now lively with chatter. Even Mordechai's scowling presence was not enough to dissuade the students from enjoying themselves.

Of course, most of the students did not seem to know *how* to enjoy themselves. The younger ones especially were prone to sitting or lying in silence as though their brains had shut off without instructions. Mordechai's band of troublemakers were often caught wandering into the forest or up the mountainside, and Landen was apprehended in the midst of running away not once but three times. After Tristan saw him limping back into the main cave following yet another of his failed escape attempts, he found he pitied the boy, as difficult as he could be. At least Landen was smart enough to protest.

Out of the whole First Division, Mei Ling and Ori were the only two who remained quiet and tense. Tristan often caught sight of Pavlina entertaining Emma and a few of the other younger students when Mordechai was away, and Rajesh loved poring over a stack of maps that Tony had amassed of the entire South Island. Another of Rajesh's favorite pastimes was trying to get Mei Ling's attention; as much as he tried talking to her and telling jokes that only he laughed at, she never once replied or even acknowledged that she was listening.

Tristan watched this all with envy; he and Amber were afraid to speak to Rajesh or each other any more than necessary, for fear someone would accuse them of scheming.

No longer were they devoting their time to lessons and homework. Almost all activities had been halted in favor of intensive magic-harvesting—they had a quota to meet before Ilana arrived, and it seemed their teachers would be in deep trouble if the target was missed.

For days at a time, ten students and two teachers would disappear on a long hike to the nearest glacier to harvest water magic. Surely there had to be an easier way, but this was the only one Ilana knew. The First Division was never selected for that particular duty—Tony admitted that his students were too valuable to risk. Stefan was no longer teaching the First Division; he stood in for Ilana in her absence, and had already become nearly as harsh and unforgiving as her.

Several times a week, Tristan's division would spend the day deep in the caves, chiseling likely-looking crystals from the wall and siphoning auras from stalagmites. It was Pavlina who had come up with this brilliant idea, and after a great deal of testing, they discovered that stalactites and stalagmites would release magic if they were tapped like a maple tree. Their vapor content was so high that two marbles instead of one would often congeal in the plastic bottles they were now using to trap magic. Occasionally one would shatter, which made Tristan wince. He hated seeing the beautiful shapes destroyed.

One day his division was deep in the cave, harvesting a section of finger-sized stalactites interspersed with glowworms on the ceiling, when he found himself alone in a side chamber with Pavlina. He had never spoken a word to her before.

"What do you think about Ilana?" he asked in a low voice.

Pavlina jumped, dropping her water bottle. The lid popped off and vapor spilled out. "Look what you did," she said coldly. "Why do you want to know about Ilana? Is this a trick?"

"I'm not trying to mess with you."

Bending down, Pavlina retrieved her water bottle and tucked a strand of coarse blonde hair behind one ear. "We should rejoin the others."

"Wait," Tristan said. "Have you always lived with Ilana? Do you remember where you came from?"

"Of course I do," she snapped. "If you want to know, Ilana stole me off my Baba Sofiyko when I was seven. Baba had a stroke, and when I ran off to get help, Ilana grabbed me. Are you happy now?"

She turned and marched away, leaving Tristan in the dark, the dying batteries in his headlamp hardly bright enough to illuminate the water bottle in his hands. Of course, he had expected this. Why should anyone trust him? This school was their family, their home, and he was a stranger who had come to take that all away.

As he gathered his empty water bottles and clambered down the rocky shelf to rejoin the group before his flashlight died, he realized that Pavlina had given him a sign. She was not happy here; she was terrified to speak openly against Ilana, but brave enough to admit that she did not believe the lies she had been fed. He just needed to speak to her again when the time was right, and approach it more delicately the next time around. *Imagine how you'd feel if Blake started telling you Alldusk was evil.*

For the first time in years, Ilana's students had hours of free time at night. It grew dark around six this time of year, so they ate early dinners and spent the evening lounging around in the main cavern or just outside the cave. Rules had slackened, though Tristan still felt Mordechai's eyes on him whenever he strayed from the main chamber. At first the students didn't seem to know what to do with their spare time. Most of them—the younger ones especially—lay on their bed-rolls and stared at the high cavern roof until they fell asleep. Blake and Ricardo started challenging different boys to wrestling matches on the grassy shelf outside, which Stefan did not discourage. More than one boy returned with a bloody nose or an ugly bruise across his face.

Landen and the twenty-odd kids who had been in Mordechai's care were suddenly free from wherever they had been locked up, and they seized the opportunity to cause an ungodly amount of trouble. Unharvested stalactites were cracked off with a shovel, the composting toilet was smeared three times with feces, and sleeping bags and mats were constantly going missing. Everyone evacuated the cave in a frenzy when they heard a *boom* like dynamite deep in the bowels of the earth; only when a grimy girl came running out of the cave, shrieking like a banshee with blood dripping from her hands, did they learn what had happened. She had apparently dropped a fuel canister and a smoldering stick down one of the shafts to see what happened, and the entire thing had exploded, weakening the cave walls and shredding her skin to pieces in an eruption of rocks.

Watching the girl stare defiantly at Mordechai even as he yelled at her, heedless of the blood now staining her shirt, Tristan filed the idea away as a good way to detonate the marbles they would need to destroy the globe.

In the confused aftermath, Tristan beckoned Amber and Rajesh into a narrow, high-ceilinged side cavern to discuss their plans.

"Have you talked to anyone?" Tristan asked Rajesh.

He nodded. "Ori's game, I think, but he's a bit hard to

read sometimes. I don't think he'll report us, though… And I talked to Mei Ling, but she won't have a bit of it."

"She won't turn us in, though?"

"No," Rajesh said immediately. "She's just scared. I don't think she likes Ilana any more than I do, but she's so used to obeying that it's hard to think of anything else."

Tristan was surprised by how vehemently he defended her. Did he secretly like her? "I've talked to Pavlina," he said. "I'm not sure she'll agree, but she's not a fan of Ilana. She's just a bit touchy."

"You could say that again."

Amber said, "I have an idea."

Tristan and Rajesh looked at her eagerly.

"I think I could recreate the barrier I put over the Lair, only I would fasten it to the cave mouth instead of the globe. It doesn't allow anyone unfamiliar to pass through, so when Ilana arrives, she will be trapped outside. As she tries to figure out how to enter and move the globe into the cave, she will delay at the cave mouth long enough for us to set off a pile of marbles hidden there. The explosion will destroy the globe and possibly Ilana as well."

"Wow," Tristan said. "You've been thinking about that a lot!"

Amber smiled shyly. "I feel as though this is my responsibility. Stefan will call on me to help with the barrier, so this will be the perfect way for me to do my part."

"How do we get enough marbles?" Rajesh asked. "And where do we put them?"

"It's easier to steal marbles than you'd think," Tristan said. "Especially with Ilana away. We'll have to dig a hole and start hiding them outside. Maybe we can make a trapdoor or something."

"Out of what?"

Tristan shrugged. "I'll figure it out. Leave that to me. I'll get the hole dug this week, and then we can start hiding marbles. We'll take turns going to the toilet in the middle of the night, and we can add a few marbles each time." He glanced at Rajesh. "You think Ori will help? The more people, the better. They'll notice if we start sneaking off every third night."

"He will," Rajesh said. "No guarantees he won't turn around and betray us someday, but right now he'd be happy to help."

"Right." That would have to do for now. "I'll talk to Pavlina again. Even five of us is a lot better than three. We'll have plenty of marbles by the time Ilana gets here. Amber, will you start working on the barrier?"

"Okay. Stefan already asked me to help with it, so I'll just change it to keep Ilana out."

"You haven't already started it, have you?" he asked in surprise.

Amber looked away. "Just two days ago. I didn't want to get your hopes up—I'm afraid it won't work."

Footsteps were crunching across the cave floor as the students returned, so Tristan, Amber, and Rajesh slipped back into the main hallway before anyone noticed their absence. Mordechai was dragging the scrawny girl down a steeply-sloping side passage; her hands had been hastily bandaged with strips of someone's shirt.

While the other students settled down to their usual nightly routines—some lying motionless as always, others playing cat's cradle with a set of ropes, still others braiding each other's hair—Tristan settled against the wall near their food stash, looking around for anything that could function as a trapdoor.

Their supplies were still painfully limited. Despite several trips to the nearest town for resupply, they were still eating canned beans, pasta with canned tomato sauce, and lentils and rice, all cooked on a mix of tiny backpacking stoves and larger square camping stoves. There were pots and pans he could ostensibly steal, but their absence would be noticed.

Getting to his feet, he edged toward the cavern entrance, where he crawled through the narrow gap into the main hallway. In a side chamber just below the composting toilet lay their dump-heap, which was carried out in pieces each time another group hiked out for more supplies. Most of it was comprised of empty cans and cardboard boxes, with a few empty gas canisters added to the mix. He sifted through the junk, grateful that most of it had been cleaned before being discarded. Near the bottom he found a narrow sheet of corrugated metal which looked as though it had been hewn from the roof of the composting toilet. It was longer and skinnier than he would have liked, but it would work better than a heap of mangled cans.

With a jagged rock, he banged at the metal until he had

weakened it enough to bend it sideways along one of the grooves. Then he folded it back and forth until the crease snapped in two. Hiding one of the halves under his shirt—not the best idea, as the edges threatened to tear at his skin—he crept from the junk-room, wary of discovery.

No one stopped him on his way to the mouth of the cave, where the sun had just dropped below the nearest mountaintop. To the left of the entrance stood a clump of bushes, and it was here that Tristan measured out a line in the ground where he would dig. Once the outline was scratched in the dirt, he hid the metal under a rock and returned to the main cavern before anyone noticed his absence.

Stefan was waiting for him, arms folded to emphasize the bulk of his muscles. "Where have you been?"

"I'm not allowed to walk around outside?" Tristan asked innocently.

"Not on my watch."

Good thing he had hidden the corrugated metal outside rather than under his mat, which he'd considered. "What about Blake and Ricardo? Are you going to start locking them inside, too?"

Lowering his voice, Stefan hissed, "You know perfectly well that Ilana will have my head if anything goes wrong. Especially where you and Amber are concerned. If you're going to start disregarding my orders, you might as well hang me and get it over with."

A niggling feeling of guilt tugged at Tristan, but he ignored it. Stefan had been in Ilana's pocket for too long.

"Don't worry," he said coolly. "Ilana won't have anything to complain about."

Defiantly, he stepped around Stefan.

As he sank onto his sleeping mat, he realized that several pairs of eyes had followed him across the cavern. He had just stood up to a teacher and gotten away with it. They *envied* him.

The following morning, Stefan and Amber were both absent for several hours after breakfast. Several other teachers were gone as well, so Tristan assumed they were working on the new barrier.

He and the rest of the First Division spent the time seated around a campfire built atop a flat rock as large as a table, where they collected fire magic by throwing scraps of bark and dried leaves into the flames. It was Tristan's favorite time here—the flames helped ease the chill that had settled deep in his bones, and the familiar smell of wood smoke brought back wonderful memories of bonfires at the Lair.

"I wonder where Ilana's at now," Blake said off-handedly, scooping up two jarfuls of vapor with a flourish.

"A month away still," Ricardo said with a twinge of annoyance. "And Amber's going to be her new favorite student by the end of that, not you."

"That freak?" Blake snorted. "You wish."

"Well, she's the one putting up the new barrier, dimwit. And rumor has it that she's helped Ilana gather *air magic*."

Tristan's grip on his jar tightened. Who had told them

that? Not Rajesh, surely?

But Rajesh was pointedly ignoring Blake and Ricardo, who were widely acknowledged to be good-for-nothing showoffs.

"You're just jealous," Blake said, flexing his biceps as he screwed on the cap of his jar.

"Blake thinks he'll be promoted to teaching when Ilana gets back," Rajesh whispered dismissively.

Blake shot him a warning look. "I'll crush you someday. Watch your step."

"That's why I don't wrestle," Rajesh said. "I'm not an idiot."

"Oh, knock it off," Tony said, stretching his arms over his head.

Blake, Ricardo, and Rajesh subsided into a disgruntled silence. Gazing out at the dark sea of beech trees below, Tristan reflected that Ilana's death wouldn't come close to mitigating the harm that these magicians could cause. He would have a set of very dangerous enemies before long— Blake and Mordechai alone could finish him off, and as powerful as Amber was, she couldn't fight close to a hundred impeccably-trained magicians. Almost every one of them could draw on their own power, a skill which remained a major handicap for Tristan. He had drawn on his own strength once, and another time on the forest's power, but it had been a long time since he had managed either.

Even Helene, the tiny Norwegian girl who had first summoned him to the cafeteria, could probably overpower him when it came to magic.

When noon came, the sun pale behind a thin sheath of clouds, Tony left the fire smoldering for the next division to use and led the way back to the cave for lunch. Tristan tapped Pavlina on the arm; with a sigh, she bent over and pretended to tie her shoe so she lagged behind the class.

"I know what you want from me," she said flatly. "You're going to try something, aren't you? You and Rajesh. I've seen you scheming together."

"Maybe we are," he said in a low voice. "Would you join us?"

"No," she said at once. "I won't report you, but it's too dangerous. You should know that."

"What if it meant stopping Ilana? What if we could save everyone?"

"I'm not a hero," Pavlina said. "You've got the wrong person."

"I'm not, either," Tristan said desperately. "But I'm doing this because I have to. Because no one else can."

The rest of the division had already reached the cave. Looking over his shoulder, Tony noticed that he was missing two of his students and waved them over.

Pavlina straightened. "I'm sorry. I can't help you."

"Fine. But I'm not giving up yet." Tristan watched her go, fanning smoke away from his face. He wasn't very good at persuasion; where was Rusty when he needed him? Disgruntled, he started after Pavlina.

That night, Tristan sneaked out with a trowel that had served as their original toilet and, shivering in the fierce breeze, began digging out the pit for their marbles. He uprooted a hunk of soil and grass, which he laid carefully atop his corrugated metal lid. Then he started digging deeper, forming a narrow rectangular hole that would barely have fit his two feet, one in front of the other.

A morepork owl called from nearby as he worked, the distinctive *ru-ru* sound moving from branch to branch, and clouds scudded across the face of the moon.

He lost track of the time as he worked, enjoying the simple labor and the solitude. Over an hour passed before a rustle in the bushes startled him from his daze.

Dropping the trowel, he whirled, but it must have been nothing more than a mouse or a possum. Nervous now, he fitted the metal top over the rough hole, arranged the dirt and grass convincingly over the top so he couldn't see where the ground had been disturbed, and hurried back into the cave. He deposited the trowel behind a sack of rice and crept to his bed, trying not to step on anyone or blind anyone with his headlamp.

"You're crazy," Pavlina whispered from two mats over.

Tristan wriggled into his sleeping bag, only then noticing how cold his extremities had grown. "Are you sure you don't want to help?"

"*Yes!*"

His hands still smelled of dirt and rusting metal. Tucking them under his arms to warm his fingers, he tried to sleep. Pavlina was right. They were completely insane if they thought this would actually work.

In the morning, Pavlina cornered Tristan on his way back from the toilet and said, "I've changed my mind. I'll help you. But only if you swear you'll be careful."

Tristan was taken aback. "Of course! Why did you change your mind?"

"Something Mordechai said." She gave him an icy look. "Don't mess this up."

"I won't."

She left Tristan feeling a bit rattled. His promise felt empty. He couldn't *not* mess things up; this whole endeavor was almost guaranteed to turn into a disaster. At least he had one more ally to call upon.

"She'll help us," he whispered to Rajesh on their walk down to a new cavern to harvest stalagmites. Tony had given every third student an extra-powerful flashlight, which did not entirely cut through the gloom; they were heading into a less-explored section of the cave today, which meant they had to keep a sharp eye out for bottomless shafts and loose rocks.

"I'm impressed," Rajesh said under his breath. "I wouldn't have even tried her, if you'd left it to me."

"I've dug the hole, too. I'll show you where it is tonight."

Rajesh turned his flashlight down to reveal a pothole that opened into a black abyss. "Careful. Does that mean we're collecting marbles now?"

"Yeah." Tristan pressed his back to the wall as he sidled around the dark pit. He wasn't going anywhere near that. Compared to this, the unfinished tunnels in the Lair seemed safe and familiar. As a breath of air stirred from the depths of the cave, goosebumps slithered up his arms.

"What're you whispering about, traitor?" Ricardo hissed from behind Tristan.

"Trying to decide if we should push you down that hole."

Ricardo shoved him in the back so hard that he lost his balance and toppled forward, grazing his knees on the rough stones.

"Watch where you're going, scar-face," Ricardo spat, kicking Tristan in the ribs as he passed him.

Blake stepped on Tristan's pinky as he followed Ricardo. Once the group had passed, Tristan stood and brushed dirt from his jeans. His left knee stung. Hurrying to catch up to Mei Ling, who followed at the back of their division, he wondered if Ricardo and Blake had always been like this, or if they had kept their heads down and minded their own business until now, biding their time.

By the time they reached the new cavern, which was dripping with more stalactites than Tristan had ever seen in one place before, he was feeling more than a little claustrophobic. The tunnel had narrowed, the ceiling so low that they had to crawl at times, and the stale, musty air was thick enough to taste.

"This would be a real winner if they ever found it." Tony shone his light around the walls, illuminating a great clump of stalagmites that formed what looked like a great spiky throne. Ribbons of cave bacon, striped and translucent, girded the far wall, and a small pool lay in the center. "Don't break anything. I'll skin you alive if anything happens."

"The entire aura of that formation is contained in one piece," Amber said, pointing to the throne-like mass growing from the floor. She had never spoken out in class before.

Tony joined her. "You mean the whole bloody thing'll come gushing out as soon as we tap it?"

She nodded. "If we turn off our lights, we can all collect pieces of it. We might be able to get twenty or thirty marbles out of there."

"I'll surrender to your expertise," Tony joked. "C'mon, guys, we don't have all day."

The rest of the First Division clustered around the clump of stalagmites, infusing the formation with a golden halo from their flashlights and headlamps.

"Would you like to do the honors, Amber?" He handed her the delicate pick with its hollow center.

She waited until everyone had their jars ready. This was the only brand of magic Stefan had deemed valuable enough to use their precious glass jars on; fire and water magic were fine in plastic bottles. "We should turn off the lights," she said. "It will be easier to spot the aura in the dark."

Tristan switched off his headlamp at once, and the others reluctantly followed suit. Blake was the last to turn off his flashlight, eyeing Amber with deep mistrust. In the darkness, a smattering of glowworms suddenly came to life across the ceiling.

"Ready?" Amber asked.

A murmur of assent ran through the group.

Tristan heard a faint tapping, and he leaned closer, brushing against someone's elbow. Silence hung in the air for a long moment.

Then, with a final *crunch*, green light billowed from the rock. The aura twisted and flickered like the Northern Lights, illuminating the ghostly surface of the sculpted limestone.

Caught up in wonder, Tristan almost forgot he was supposed to capture the green vapor. Shaking himself, he reached for the top of the cloud and scooped a swath of green light into his jar. Capping the jar, he watched the others catching pieces of the magic cloud. It was an ethereal scene, the light playing across the cave formations while a cluster of glowworms shone like stars overhead.

Most of the students reached for the densest part of the vapor, though Amber quickly filled three jars with the trailing tendrils of haze, her face ghostly in the green light. That was his one advantage over these students, Tristan realized—he could not use magic with the ease they could, but he could see auras far better than most. It seemed a useless gift, but perhaps he could find a way to use it to his advantage.

At last the green vapor dissipated. Silence hung in the air long after the last jar had been capped and sealed.

Finally, with a sigh, Tony switched on his flashlight once more. "Cheers, Amber. That was a day's worth of magic right there."

Pavlina turned on her headlamp next, staring at the stalagmite throne with longing.

"Let's keep this a secret," Tony said. "We'll harvest everything we can today, and the others don't have to know a thing."

"You've been here before, haven't you?" Tristan asked as the others dispersed.

Tony gave him a sad smile. "I grew up in Nelson. My mum *hated* when I went off caving, but I was obsessed. I started exploring this cave when I was ten, and by the time I was sixteen, I could find my way through most of it in the dark."

"Why'd you join Ilana?" Tristan whispered.

Tony shot him a look of warning. "You're treading on dangerous grounds here, young mister." Twisting the flashlight on and off in his hands, he said, "I was in Europe on my OE. Spent a year in Barcelona, practicing my really awful *español*, and then headed up to London to visit family. That's when I met her." His eyes grew distant at the memory. "She's a good ten years older than me, but holy crap was she beautiful. Yes—I, being a complete fool, promised I'd do anything for her. And she's never forgotten that promise."

"What's an OE?"

"Short for Overseas Experience," Tony said. "It's what all of us Kiwis and Aussies do. See a bit of the world before we tie ourselves down. I wish I'd bloody well stayed in Barcelona." He blinked and seemed to remember suddenly where he was. "Get back to work. I can't keep talking treason or someone'll finish me off."

As Tristan selected a hollow pickaxe and went to harvest more auras, his mind was still far away. How many of the teachers regretted joining Ilana? And how many students remembered a better life before she had taken them in?

If Drakewell had his way, he would wipe out the entire school's population just to be safe. But Tristan couldn't do it. Ilana had to be stopped, that much was certain, and Mordechai was, if anything, even worse. But the rest of them...

Was Stefan hiding his resentment of Ilana behind his harsh demeanor? Did tiny Helene remain silent because she was afraid, or because she had been trained to obey? And would Emma lose her childish innocence as she grew older, or did she have a spark of independence that could never be extinguished?

Five more jars joined his collection as he mulled over the question of who was genuinely loyal to Ilana. Was it worth sacrificing her innocent followers to ensure the Lair was safe?

Of course, it was bigger than that. The whole world was at risk if Ilana wasn't stopped soon, and Tristan couldn't afford to be soft-hearted if it jeopardized their mission.

On the walk back, he followed the group in a daze, still thinking deeply about what Tony had said. The aura they had released from that cluster of stalagmites had been so beautiful, so hypnotic, that it felt like something out of another world—he suspected Tony had brought them down to that particular cave for a reason, and it had nothing to do with the amount of magic available for harvesting.

He was still walking as though half asleep when someone shoved him to the side. He stumbled two steps to his right as Blake said, "Whoops!"

The ground dropped out from under his feet.

He had stepped right into the empty shaft.

Chapter 10

What Lies Beneath

Tristan screamed, arms flailing wildly as he plummeted into the darkness.

As he howled, fear blinding him, something deep within him stirred. The air rushing past slowed as he yanked a burst of power from inside him.

A fierce gale swept up from the depths of the cave, slamming into him. It supported his weight, and little by little, tossed about on the wind, he was lowered to the bottom of the pit.

At last the wind stilled. Thoroughly shaken, Tristan lay on the uneven ground, staring at the tiny circle of light far above. He felt drained, his entire body bruised and wrung out, his vision swimming with haze.

"Tristan!" a voice called from far away.

It was Amber.

"I'm—down here," he shouted back, winded.

"I'll—"

Her voice faded to emptiness.

* * *

When Tristan regained consciousness, every inch of his body screamed in pain, only slightly dulled by the numbing cold. His headlamp was still glowing softly, though it had dimmed in the hours he had lain unconscious. Soon it would die, and he would be left in absolute darkness.

Where had the others gone? Had they abandoned him to his fate?

Why hadn't Amber saved him?

Beside him lay the shattered remains of one of the jars he had been carrying. He must have dropped the other one in the passageway far above.

The bottom of this hole was less than two paces wide, though when he looked around a second time, he spotted a narrow slot leading off in a different direction. Praying his headlamp didn't die on him, he stood gingerly and turned sideways to squeeze through the slot. His muscles screamed at the movement. This hurt more than any strength training session he had ever done, though he could see at once that physical strength would help mitigate the damage caused by such a reckless use of magic.

On the other side of the slot, the tunnel widened once more, the air of this cavern staler and thicker than the one he had just left. As Tristan started walking cautiously down the corridor, his muscles protesting with each step, he found that he was oddly triumphant. He had used his own magic again, and this time he had done something incredible.

Of course, that did nothing to help the fact that he was

trapped in the depths of the Bulmer cave system with a dying flashlight and hardly enough warm layers to get him through the night.

Afraid that his headlamp would die at any moment, Tristan kept a careful eye on the passageway, looking for any side tunnels or pits that would trip him up if he lost the light. There were no diversions from the main route, though, aside from a few twisting side-passages close to the height of his head.

As he rounded a corner, he heard a faint trickling sound like a small stream flowing through the cave. He found the source of the noise before long—instead of hitting solid rock, his foot fell through the darkness and splashed into a puddle of water. Standing ankle-deep in the black water, he could feel the gentle stirring of a current. The wall to his right was wet; evidently the water was seeping down the rock and then flowing through the cave. Which meant there had to be a back exit of some sort.

Now his flashlight had reached its last minutes of life. The beam was hardly bright enough to illuminate his hands on the cave walls. Turning and stepping out of the stream, he started back the way he had come, his right sock squishing with each step. Ten steps later, the flashlight was nothing more than an irritating halo of light on his forehead, so he switched it off and continued blindly. A more complete darkness he had never known—at once he felt suffocated and vertiginous, as though an endless drop waited before him and narrow walls were beginning to press in around him.

When he reached the narrow slot, he panicked for a moment, unable to figure out which way was forward. Trying to steady his breathing, he groped around the walls in search of a way through. At last he felt a narrow gap in the rock, farther to the left than he had remembered, and he slotted his shoulders into the opening, squeezing his hips through as an afterthought. It was very eerie down here with no light; he couldn't help but imagine he was sliding into his own tomb in a musty catacomb. The whole world could have ceased to exist up above, and he would never know.

As soon as he escaped into the round chamber at the bottom of the pit, he let out his breath.

Someone would find him eventually. Amber wouldn't just leave him down here. She must have been forced to continue with the class, but she wouldn't leave him down here for too long.

Would she?

There was nothing to do but wait. If the night passed without any sign of a rescuer, he would return the way he'd come and follow the underground stream to its exit.

Sinking down with his back against the uneven limestone wall, he wrapped his arms around his knees for warmth, his muscles still aching. Before he knew it, he had fallen into a doze.

He woke with a start to the sound of his name.

"Tristan! Where are you? Turn on your headlamp!"

It was Rajesh. His voice echoed oddly down the shaft, much farther away than he had realized.

"Tristan! I can see you down there." This time it was Amber who called.

Scrambling to his feet, Tristan shouted, "My headlamp is dead! Do you have a rope?"

"Yeah," Rajesh called back. His head appeared over the hole, face glowing in the light of a flashlight. "But how are you going to find it in the dark?"

"I'll figure it out," Tristan said.

A loud clanging echoed down the pit, metal thudding against metal, and after the sound had died away, Amber dropped a bundle of rope down the shaft. The rope uncoiled as it fell, disappearing beyond the reach of her headlamp, but Tristan heard it strike the floor beside him with a soft *whump*. He waved his hands before him until he found the rope, which he grasped like a lifeline.

"You ready?" he called. Even raising his hands over his head made his muscles scream.

"It's bolted into the ground," Rajesh shouted back. "You're good to go."

Hand over hand, Tristan began hauling himself up, blindly walking his feet up the wall and seeking purchase on the smooth limestone surface. People in movies made this look so easy; just a few feet off the ground, his arms were shaking from the effort of holding the rope, and his palms were raw and sweaty.

Slowly, ever so slowly, the light at the top of the hole grew closer. When he paused and risked glancing up, he could make out Amber's wide eyes and Rajesh's worried frown illuminated in the single flashlight.

Stopping had been a mistake. When he started hauling himself up again, his arms felt like they had turned to jelly. He was going to drop the rope; any second now he would go plummeting back into the darkness.

"I can't go much farther," he said. "Can you pull me up?"

Amber and Rajesh took hold of the rope, vanishing from the circle of light as they positioned themselves. All at once the wall was grazing Tristan's knees as he soared upward faster than he had been climbing. He clung desperately to the rope as he was dragged to the top of the pit; Amber and Rajesh only stopped when his hands had reached the rim.

"Can you pull yourself up?" Rajesh asked. "I don't want to hurt you."

Tristan kicked at the wall until he found a small slot for his feet. Straightening his legs, he heaved his body up until his chest flopped onto solid ground again. He rested for a moment, panting and bent double, until he had summoned up the strength to haul his legs over the lip of the hole onto the cave floor.

Cursing under his breath, he rolled over and stared at the ceiling. It was so good to see again.

"Sorry we took so long," Rajesh said, kneeling beside Tristan and untying the rope from a bolt he had driven into the cave floor. "I didn't know you were missing until we got back to the main cave. Stefan wouldn't let us go off searching for you, but after dinner Tony slipped us a rope and that bolt, and Amber knew exactly where you were."

"Tony seems like a decent person," Amber said.

Tristan nodded. "I was talking to him earlier today. He wishes he'd never joined Ilana. I bet he'd help us if he had the chance."

"Don't count on it," Rajesh said. "He won't turn us in, but he definitely won't stand up against Ilana." He helped Tristan to his feet. "I chucked a few marbles into that hole you dug, by the way. We went looking for it on our way down here. You did a good job with it."

"Thanks," Tristan said. "I lost a couple marbles down there. The jars shattered when I fell."

"Whatever," Rajesh said. "We got plenty today. Tony won't notice if any went missing."

"Are you okay?" Amber asked. "You must have done a powerful spell to keep yourself safe."

Tristan lifted his chin with pride. "I didn't know what I was doing, but somehow I summoned up a big gust of wind that stopped me from falling. I passed out afterwards, though. And now everything hurts like hell."

"Very impressive," Amber said, giving him a brilliant smile.

Rajesh looped the rope over his arm. "Come on. Let's get back before the teachers decide they'd rather do without us anyway."

As they started back along the tunnel, Amber leading in the dark while Tristan wore her headlamp, Tristan glanced back at Rajesh. "You shouldn't have come after me, you know. I'm glad you did, but the others won't forget that you helped me."

"I don't care," Rajesh said. "They'll figure it out soon enough. As soon as Ilana gets here."

"If they don't catch us sneaking out every night first," Tristan said.

"Speaking of which," Rajesh said, "I talked to Pavlina. She'll start stealing marbles for us tomorrow. We can take turns hiding them, once every five days."

"Perfect," Tristan said. "Be careful, though. We've stolen marbles before, and it's easy to accidentally take too many. They'll notice if the bottles aren't producing as many as before."

"You stole marbles before?" Rajesh sounded impressed. "Not from Ilana, did you?"

Tristan shook his head. "No way. When we first started at the Lair, none of us knew what the marbles were being used for. We were afraid the teachers were doing something horrible, so we started hoarding our own marbles in case we needed to fight them someday."

"And now you've agreed to risk your lives for them?"

"We're not just doing it for them," Tristan said. "Ilana has to be stopped, and we were the only ones she wanted to recruit."

When they reached the cave entrance once more, Tristan and Rajesh lagged behind while Amber slipped into the main cave.

"I'll pretend I wasn't with you guys," Tristan said. "Go on."

He waited another ten minutes before crawling through the gap into the tunnel; when he dropped to his knees, he gasped in pain as his raw skin began to bleed once more. Blake looked up from his dinner in surprise, though his incredulity soon turned into a taunting smile. He had gotten away with his little prank, and had nearly killed Tristan in the process.

Tristan scraped up the last of the lentil-rice stew from the bottom of one of the camping pots, spooning globs of it into his metal cup before retreating to his bedroll to eat. Blake looked up at him with a knowing sneer, but the other students hardly spared him a glance. As warmth began to return to his stiff limbs, the ache in his knees intensified. He gritted his teeth and tried to ignore it until he had finished his dinner; at last he gave up and went in search of band-aids and antibacterial cream.

Tony was inspecting their day's haul of marbles from his seat near the first-aid kit.

"You okay?" he asked in an undertone.

Tristan nodded.

"Stefan wouldn't let anyone go after you. I told him Ilana would be furious if you vanished, but he wouldn't have a word of it. Miserable bugger."

"It's fine. We didn't come here to win Stefan's friendship."

Tony studied Tristan, who stuck two band-aids to each knee with unwonted concentration. "You're playing a very dangerous game, young man."

"I know what I'm doing," Tristan said. "And I don't want to get you involved."

Getting to his feet, he shoved the paper scraps into his

pocket. "I'm glad you took over our division, though." He left Tony in the corner, examining the magic vapor that was just now congealing into green marbles. One of the jars held six marbles—Tristan knew whose that had to be.

The next two weeks passed far too quickly. Ilana drew closer by the day, and in the meantime they had only managed to stash fifty-odd marbles in the hole beside the cave mouth. It would hardly be enough to cause even a minor explosion. Amber was making good progress with the barrier, though. The frame had almost entirely taken shape, and all that remained was infusing it with magic so it would expand to guard the entrance to their cavern. Stefan would have preferred to seal off the entire cave mouth, but Tony pointed out that a bunch of tourists would notice if the cave that had starred as the Mines of Moria in Lord of the Rings suddenly vanished off the slopes of Mount Owen. And media attention was exactly what had ruined everything the first time around.

"Can you distract them with the barrier for a while?" Tristan asked Amber when she announced that the frame was done at last. "We need more marbles. I have to take some from the main pile, or we'll never get enough in time."

"I can try," she said, pushing her dinner around on her plate. "There is a way to change it so animals and people with weaker auras are still able to pass through, and I can ask everyone to join me outside to help." She looked terrified at the thought.

"Would you?" Tristan asked. "That would be amazing."

"Don't steal the marbles yourself," Amber said urgently. "You'll get caught. Ask one of the others to help you."

"I'll see," Tristan said. He felt guilty asking anyone to take that risk.

"Tomorrow afternoon," Amber said. "I'll do it then. Make sure you use the time well. When do they think Ilana will arrive?"

"Ten days from now," Tristan said flatly. "We're dead."

Amber bit her lip. "We've gotten too far to give up now. We can only try our best. Tomorrow."

Tristan grimaced at her. Ever since that first week in New Zealand, he had barely had a minute alone with her. Even now, they were sitting off in a corner of the main cavern with their dinners on their knees, trying not to appear too much like they were scheming. That night up on the ice sheet was beginning to seem like nothing more than a dream.

He wanted to tell her how much he missed going for walks with her, how desperately he wished everyone else would just disappear, but their mission had consumed them both.

As soon as Rajesh heard their plan, he volunteered to steal as many marbles as he could get away with while Amber distracted the rest of the school.

"They already suspect you," Tristan said. "It'd really be better if one of the others did it."

"You think *Pavlina* is going to risk her life for us?" Rajesh made a face. "She hardly agreed to join us. And I don't trust Ori."

"Why not?"

Rajesh glanced at the other side of the room, where Ori was bouncing a rubber-band ball off the wall again and again. "He's completely closed-off. Hasn't revealed a thing since the day he arrived here—he won't even talk to me now. I don't know anything about his past, his family, his *anything*. He could be an alien for all we know."

"At least that means he won't talk, right? He seems trustworthy enough."

"You think too highly of everyone," Rajesh said drily. "You're a fool to have trusted any of us."

"You've already proved that wrong," Tristan said. "It's your choice—you or Ori. I'd do it myself, but Stefan's going to notice if I'm missing."

The following afternoon, right after lunch, Amber disappeared in the company of Stefan, Amelia, and two other teachers Tristan didn't know. Before long, Stefan returned to summon the rest of the students onto the grassy shelf outside the cave.

"The barrier will go up tomorrow," he announced. "Amber has suggested that we should program it to exclude any unfamiliar magicians but still allow tourists through. We have to acquaint it with our auras."

It sounded like nonsense to Tristan; he had a funny

feeling that Amber was just messing with Stefan. He followed the crowd through the narrow exit, unable to spot any of his allies in the melee. When he emerged into the sunlight, he spotted Pavlina, Ricardo, Blake, and Mei Ling, though as far as he could tell, Rajesh and Ori were both missing.

"Where's Rajesh?" Blake asked pointedly, looking Tristan's way.

He knew. He must have seen Rajesh helping Amber save him from the pit.

"Helene, please go fetch Rajesh," Amelia said.

The tiny blonde girl turned mechanically and headed back into the shadow of the cave. Before she had disappeared around the corner, a shadow emerged.

"I'm here," Rajesh said. "Sorry. I lost my shoes."

It was Ori who would be doing their dirty work, then. Tristan had spoken with confidence, but he hardly knew Ori. He had no idea whether or not he was to be trusted.

"Good," Stefan said with mild irritation. "Let's begin."

Forming a line that circled around the flat space, they approached what looked like an intricately-woven basket and took turns infusing it with their auras. It could be that this would exclude everyone who was not currently present from passing through the barrier, or it could be a farce designed for distraction and nothing more. Just after Tristan had taken his turn, Ori sidled out of the cave to join the line, his forehead damp with perspiration.

For better or worse, the job was done.

It wasn't until late that night that Tristan got

confirmation of Ori's work. Rajesh challenged Tristan to a game of chess with a makeshift board drawn on a flattened cardboard box, and as they were setting up, he whispered, "He's done it. They're in a pair of boxes in the dump-heap." He raised his voice. "That's supposed to be a bishop, not the king. See the pointy hat?"

Tristan raised his eyebrows at the dried-up mushroom he was using as a chess piece. "Which one's the king, then?"

"That funny piece of bark."

The game ended quickly—Tristan won, to his surprise, though that might have been because he couldn't tell the difference between his queen and his left-hand castle.

"Nine days until Ilana's here," Rajesh said offhandedly as they swept the remaining chess pieces off the cardboard box.

"It's not enough time." Tristan crawled into his sleeping bag, searching the room for Amber, Pavlina, and Ori, who were each wrapped up in their own pursuits—Amber was lying on her back and studying the glowworms with fierce concentration, Pavlina was reading something she must have picked up at an airport, and Ori was braiding a set of thin cords together. "I shouldn't have dragged you into this. Any of you."

Rajesh ran a hand through his short hair. "I'm glad you did. I would've snapped someday if you hadn't, and they would've killed me."

The following night, Tristan waited until several hours had

gone by since the last person had stirred. Then, holding his breath, he slipped out of his unzipped sleeping bag and tiptoed along the narrow gap between mats, trusting the glowworms to light his way. He couldn't afford to turn on his flashlight.

Outside, he let out his breath and made for the trash heap, where he rummaged through boxes and cans and plastic wrap until he found a mangled cereal-box that weighed more than it should have. Inside, more than a hundred gold, green, and blue marbles were packed close together.

Cradling the box in his arms, he crept to the cave mouth, where the moon seemed as bright as daylight after the darkness of the cavern. He wondered if he was beginning to acquire Amber's ability to see in the dark; when he had first arrived in New Zealand, he was almost certain the glowworms had not cast enough light to see by.

The rectangular hole was as well-hidden as always. Scanning the clearing for any sign of movement, he dropped to his knees, lifted the corrugated metal lid, and dumped the entire box of marbles into the depths of the hole. It was getting close to half-full now; they were still miles from finishing, but with any luck they would be able to do some damage with what they had here.

Leaving the night as still as ever, Tristan sneaked back into the cave to retrieve the second box of marbles. This one took more digging than the first, but at last he shoved aside a worn-out backpack filled with rocks and found a square box that had once held a set of camping pots. It was twice as heavy as the first box—Ori had done a brilliant job.

Outside, he knelt and added this second pile to the first. The stash of marbles nearly doubled as he overturned this box, and he winced at the clatter.

Then something caught his attention.

Footsteps.

After a pause, a scrawny figure emerged from the cave with a backpack on his shoulders that had been stuffed near to bursting.

It was Landen. Tristan had nearly forgotten about the irritating kid from the plane. "Where are you going?" he whispered.

"Nowhere," Landen said coldly.

"You're not running away, are you?"

"What's it to you? You won't report me. What're you doing, anyway? Doesn't look right." He crept closer and peered into the hole Tristan had dug.

"Nothing."

"Can I help?"

"No. If you want to run away, go." Tristan grabbed the trowel he had left under the bushes and started scraping dirt over the marbles.

"Are you sure I can't help?"

"*Yes!* Now get away from here!"

Landen gave Tristan a spiteful look. "You'll wish you hadn't said that."

"What d'you—"

Opening his mouth, Landen gave a horrible, inhuman

scream that startled a few bats hanging in the cave entrance. As the bats took wing, Landen turned and sprinted off into the darkness, his backpack clanging with each footfall.

A second too late, Tristan realized he couldn't hide the marbles in time. Someone was already approaching the cave mouth, headlamp splitting the darkness. Throwing his trowel aside, Tristan kicked the trapdoor closed and straightened, pretending to do up his fly.

"What are you doing out here, boy?"

Tristan froze. It was Mordechai. "J-just watering some grass," he mumbled.

"Like hell you were. Get away from there." With one beefy hand, he shoved Tristan away from the trapdoor. Raising his voice, he yelled, "Backup! I've got trouble!"

Someone else must have heard Landen's scream, because three more figures were already emerging from the cave mouth as he shouted. Another ten came scrambling up behind them; before long the entire school's population was clustered around Mordechai and Tristan, outlines blurred in the moonlight.

Tristan couldn't think straight. He had just ruined his only chance to stop Ilana; if he didn't flee, he and Amber would likely be killed. But though his feet itched to set off running into the wilderness, he stood his ground. Too much had gone into this plan to let it fall apart so easily.

"What is it?" Amelia asked, hands on her hips. "I hope you haven't made a fuss for nothing."

A hazy plan was beginning to take shape. As Mordechai dropped to his knees to feel for the trapdoor he had seen, Tristan backed into the crowd of students until he was no longer at the center of attention. Amber grabbed his sleeve.

"What now?" she breathed in his ear.

"Is that barrier ready?" he hissed.

"Yes."

"How fast can we put it up?"

She was silent for a long time. "In five minutes, if we do it right the first time."

Tristan ground his teeth in frustration. This would be impossibly dangerous, and their chances of success were so slim as to be nonexistent. But he had to try.

"Get the others into the cave," he whispered. "I'll come last."

Amber's eyes widened in understanding. She slid between Ricardo and a short girl to reach Pavlina, whose expression was as closed as always.

In the middle of the circle, Mordechai had just found the trapdoor and lifted it triumphantly free of the ground.

"That's what this must be for," Stefan said, kicking the trowel.

"What's in it?" Blake asked, shoving his way to the front of the group.

Out of the corner of his eye, Tristan saw Pavlina conferring in an undertone with Ori, who then moved off to speak to Rajesh. Ducking down, Pavlina extracted herself from the group and melted into the shadows of the cave. Amber must have been waiting there already, because there was no sign of her outside.

"Marbles," Mordechai said harshly. "*Someone* has been stealing from us." He leaned over the hole and dragged out a handful of gold marbles, which he flung across the trampled dirt.

Tristan thought it would be prudent of him to vanish before Mordechai drew attention his way once more. As the students crowded closer to the pit, he ducked between them and slipped into the cave. The shadows swallowed him at once, and no one looked his way. Breathing as softly as he could, he felt his way forward.

"Amber? Pavlina?" he whispered.

"Here," Amber said. She reached for his elbow in the dark. "We can't risk lights. Can you feel this?" She pressed the frame of the barrier into his hands. "There's Rajesh and Ori." She could see in the dark just as well as she could in broad daylight.

"Got it. Do we all have to be holding it?"

"Yes."

Another shape approached, and Tristan froze in fear.

"It's okay." The voice was soft and frightened. "I want to help."

Mei Ling? Rajesh must have grabbed her at the last minute.

"We need to hold hands, and I will direct our power into the barrier," Amber whispered. "Theoretically this should work, but—"

"Just tell us what to do," Tristan said. They were running out of time.

"Send me your power," she said. "As much as you can

spare. Use a marble if you must."

Tristan grabbed a marble from his pocket before linking hands with Amber and Rajesh; he didn't trust himself to call upon his own power. Just as he had done in the Lair, he closed his eyes, took the marble's power into himself, and sent it to Amber. Her hand grew warmer as the combined power began to build within her, until her skin was so fiery Tristan almost released his grip.

His part was done. The rest was up to Amber.

Opening his eyes, he turned to look at the clustered students just outside the cave.

"What's this about?" Tony was asking sleepily. "Why would anyone bury heaps of marbles here, anyway?"

"Ask Tristan," Mordechai growled. "He's the one I caught here. I *told* Ilana he was trouble. That bastard's had it in for us from the start."

Tristan stiffened. How much longer would Amber take?

"Where's he gone?" Stefan asked, scanning the heads of the students.

"He was just there," Mordechai said. "Find him! He must've run off. He knows we'll slaughter him if we ever see him again."

"Don't be so dramatic," Amelia said. "He's Ilana's to question. No one's getting killed tonight, understood? Students, please stay where you are. Teachers, spread out and search the hillside."

"What if he's inside the cave?" Blake asked.

"Then he's an idiot," Mordechai growled. "But go on,

search if you want."

Tristan looked desperately at Amber. Though he couldn't make out her features in the darkness, he knew she stood unmoving, the heat slowly draining from her palm.

Headlamps were turning on all throughout the crowd outside, and one outline detached itself from the group, moving towards the cave mouth.

Tristan held his breath, nerves tingling, and willed Amber to work faster.

As Blake lifted his face, his flashlight beam fell on Rajesh's feet.

Tristan tensed, ready to run if he had to.

Straightening in triumph, Blake strode forward into the cave. "I've got you! Don't even think about running." When he was close enough to cast light on every student in Tristan's circle, he turned and yelled, "Mordechai! He's here! And he's not alone." He whirled back to face Rajesh and the others. "Traitors. You'll pay for this."

"Amber," Tristan said urgently. "Amber, they're here. Are you almost done?"

Still she did not move. She might have turned to stone.

"We've got to run," Rajesh said, his face drained of color. "They'll kill us."

"Wait," Tristan said. "Don't let go yet. We have to give her a chance."

Mei Ling stared at him in horror.

Tristan wished she had saved herself and stayed outside. With one fatal decision, she had lost everything.

Mordechai was lumbering toward the cave mouth,

brandishing the muddy trowel as though he intended to use it as a weapon. Some of the younger students scattered, while a few others inched forward in curiosity.

Suddenly, he ran headlong into something that Tristan couldn't see.

With a yowl of pain, he reeled backward, nearly crushing Emma as he fell.

"What's wrong?" Stefan called from farther down the slope.

Ricardo ventured forward two steps, hand outstretched, and stopped abruptly. He slapped his hands against something in midair but could go no farther.

Drawing in a sharp breath, Tristan turned to Amber. "It worked!"

Her eyes flew open, and she released his hand. "Yes. I think it did." In the light from Blake's headlamp, he could see a faint smile growing on her lips.

All at once, Blake realized he was alone. Tristan, Rajesh, and Pavlina turned on him, and he stumbled backwards, nearly tripping over a broken stalagmite.

"Cowards," he spat. "Traitors and cowards!"

Seconds later, he had slipped past the invisible barrier onto the grass outside.

"You did it!" Tristan said. He hugged Amber and punched Rajesh in the shoulder. "I can't believe it. We're safe!"

"Apart from Blake," Amber said. "He can get through."

"Who cares?" Tristan said. "He can't hurt us."

Chapter 11

Into Darkness

Suddenly everything had turned upside down. Ilana's followers were left with nothing but the meager stash of marbles Tristan had managed to bury outside, while he, Amber, Rajesh, Pavlina, Ori, and Mei Ling had access to thousands of marbles stored in the deep wooden frame Stefan had nailed together.

The only problem was that they couldn't leave the cave without risking their lives. Several times they had gone to the cave mouth to spy on the rest of the school, and every time there had been a minimum of ten students and teachers guarding the entrance. The students on the outside could see through the barrier, but they couldn't get through no matter how hard they tried.

The rest of the school must have relocated into the forest far below, where the patchy snow didn't cover the ground, because no tents or supplies materialized on the shelf outside the cave. He assumed they would head back into Nelson and resupply at once, since they would otherwise be left with nothing but the clothes they had been wearing when Mordechai called them outside.

For the first day they spent alone in the cave, Tristan and Amber made plans with their allies and took stock of their supplies. It was such a novelty to be able to talk in the open that they piled up most of the sleeping mats together and sat in a circle simply discussing what they should do. Though he said nothing about it, Rajesh looked quietly elated; Tristan caught him grinning to himself whenever he thought no one was looking. And the source of his newfound joy was evidently Mei Ling, who had at long last given in to his persuasion. She must have been listening to his whispered commentary all along, sitting in stony silence so she could not be blamed if someone noticed his subversion.

"We've got a year's supply of food," Tristan said. "That's not a problem. And there are still twelve gas canisters here. Seven of them haven't even been used."

"The only thing we're in danger of running out of is flashlight batteries," Rajesh said. "Everyone brought their headlamps out last night, and we've only got six spares."

Tristan immediately flicked his headlamp off. "Well, we don't need them while we're just sitting here."

The others followed suit.

"Is this why you came here?" Mei Ling asked shyly. "To overthrow Ilana?"

"Yes," Amber said. "We were the only ones who stood a chance against her."

"That's so brave it's stupid," Ori said. "Ilana doesn't

just get rid of anyone who threatens her. She tortures them until they're begging to die. Then she turns them into her most loyal pets."

Pavlina made a small noise of assent. "Stefan was one of them. He may act like he cares about us, but he's lost his own free will. He would do anything Ilana asked of him in a heartbeat."

"It's true," Rajesh said. "People just don't go against Ilana. If someone even hints at rebellion, they'll vanish. Some of them return, and some of them just—don't. I don't know if she kills them right away or tortures them slowly to death, but I'm sure she enjoys it. No one would willingly risk that."

"Except all of you," Tristan said. He couldn't see the others, but he knew they listened in rapt attention. "Why did you change your minds?"

"I've been waiting for this chance all along," Rajesh said flatly. "I don't care if I die. I won't sit and pretend I agree with her any longer."

"Ilana being away has made us reckless," Mei Ling said softly. "It was a mistake to listen to you and Rajesh, but—"

"But this life isn't worth living," Ori said.

Rajesh shifted to Tristan's left. "Exactly. So, what are we going to do? We're stuck in here, and they're stuck out there. And once Ilana gets here, there's no way in hell we're getting past her. Once she's done killing everyone for disobeying her, she'll finish us off."

Tristan looked up at the glowworms for inspiration. "We have to do something they won't expect. And we *have* to destroy that globe. That's the only reason we're here. To stop Ilana."

That evening, clouds began to gather just before sunset, and a howling gale picked up overnight.

A damp chill had settled in the cavern while they slept, and when Tristan ventured to the cave mouth, he discovered a fresh blanket of snow that had robed every rock and bush in two inches of white powder. The clouds lingered through the day, soft flakes drifting down to settle on the white ground, and the students tasked with guarding the cave entrance were wrapped in every layer they owned, socks taking the place of gloves on their hands.

Even inside the cave, the temperature continued to drop several degrees as the day lengthened, the wind swirling through the low entrance to chill the main cavern, which no longer benefitted from the heat of nearly eighty bodies. Tristan and his allies spent the day huddled in their sleeping bags, only venturing out to cook meals and visit the composting toilet.

As they settled in for dinner, discouraged after a day of fruitless brainstorming, Tristan remembered something important.

"Remember when I fell down that hole?"

Rajesh laughed. "None of us are going to forget that easily."

"Well, there was a little stream down there. It must lead out somewhere, right? So there has to be a back exit."

By the light of Pavlina's single headlamp, Tristan saw

Rajesh grimace. "I really, *really* don't like tight spaces. What if we get stuck down there? What if it's such a tiny exit we can't get through, and we get lost on our way back?"

"We'll be careful," Tristan said. "Do we have any extra-long ropes we can use to guide our way?"

"Just the one we used before," Rajesh said. "All the others are tiny. They probably wouldn't stretch the length of this cavern, even if you tied them all together."

"What about that bolt you used to secure the rope? Are there more of those?"

Amber nodded. "At least ten of them, I think. Tony thought we might be rappelling deep into the cave to collect earth magic before long."

Tristan grinned. "I bet he just wanted an excuse to explore. He knows this cave inside out, apparently."

"He might know if there are any back entrances," Ori said worriedly. "You don't think he'll tell the others?"

"No." Tristan was certain of it. "He won't give us away."

The following morning, they gathered every headlamp and battery they could find and started down the widest tunnel, Tristan carrying the rope over his arm and Pavlina resting the sledgehammer on one shoulder.

"I still don't want to go down there until we know we won't get lost," Rajesh said.

"We only have six days until Ilana gets here," Tristan reminded him. "No time to lose."

"It's just another cave," Mei Ling said softly. "Why is

that one so much worse than this?"

"Because it's down at the bottom of a bloody pit," Rajesh grumbled. "You can't just walk out if you're sick of being underground."

"Fine," Tristan said. "We won't go down today. We'll set up the rope, and that's all. But we don't have time to waste. Someone has to figure out a guide-rope by tomorrow. Otherwise, I'm going down alone."

"I'm coming with you," Amber said.

Silently, Tristan thanked her for the vote of confidence.

Working together, they were able to hammer three anchors into the rock and thread the rope through all three before dropping it down the pit.

"Sure you don't want to try it out?" Tristan teased Rajesh.

"Oh, shut up."

They spent all night brainstorming, while Ori undid the twine he'd braided and tied together every scrap of rope and fabric he could dig up. It wasn't nearly enough, but the following morning Rajesh agreed to follow them into the abyss to explore.

"Five days," Tristan reminded the others as Ori started down the rope.

"That wasn't an exact date," Rajesh said. His temper had been shorter than usual these past two days; he was clearly dreading their little expedition more than he let on. "Maybe she's been delayed. Or maybe she's already here."

"If she were here, we'd know," Mei Ling said.

Her voice seemed to quiet Rajesh's fears better than anything Tristan could say. "Right. Let's get this over with." He raised his voice. "You at the bottom yet, Ori?"

"Yeah!"

Paler than usual, Rajesh grasped the rope and lowered himself over the lip of the hole. As he began inching his way down, he squeezed his eyes shut. Ten minutes passed before he called, "I'm down!"

Tristan let Mei Ling descend next, hoping her presence would keep Rajesh from panicking. When Pavlina had gone, Tristan shared a look of worry with Amber.

"This isn't going well," he whispered.

She shook her head. "Everyone knows we're traitors now. We no longer have surprise on our side."

"Do you think it'll work?"

Amber bit her lip. "I doubt it."

Tristan slid down the rope then, because he didn't want to think about their impending doom, and Amber joined him within minutes. Rajesh had tied their knotted-up assortment of strings to the end of the rope, and as soon as Amber touched the ground, he said, "Let's get this over with."

Ori led the way through the narrow slot into the passageway beyond. The whole tunnel looked much less dreary now that there were six of them filling it, their headlamps casting the curving limestone into gentle relief.

"I can hardly breathe," Rajesh whispered. "The air is so thick."

"You're just making that up," Pavlina said.

"I know what you mean," Tristan said. "It does seem mustier down here. But we're fine."

Around the next corner, their pieced-together line ran out all at once.

"That's it," Rajesh said. "I'm going back."

"The stream's just a little farther," Tristan said. "There aren't any side passages down here. Last time my headlamp was dead, and I found my way just fine."

"No way." Rajesh backed up, clutching the end of the last piece of twine. "I'm not going anywhere."

"Fine." Tristan squeezed his way to the front of the group. "We'll meet you back here, then."

Amber and the other four followed Tristan up a short rise and along a high-ceilinged passageway.

"Not much farther," Tristan said.

Though he had been expecting it, he still gave a start when his foot splashed into the stream.

"Humph. I guess we're here."

Stepping back and shaking water from his pant leg, he let the others crowd forward to take a look at the stream.

"Turn your lights off," Amber said. "I want to see if any sunlight shows through."

They obeyed, standing in silence as Amber crept forward in search of light. Tristan had a feeling she was stepping on the surface of the water now, just as she did with snow. Was there any limit to her ability to walk on water? Could she stroll across the entire ocean if she tried?

"Nothing," she said at last. "It must come out somewhere, but we'll have to follow it to see the end. And I think the water gets deeper here."

As she returned to the water's edge, Tristan turned his headlamp on again and examined the inky black pool at his feet.

"We should get back before Rajesh goes mental," Ori said wryly.

"Good point. Come on."

They retraced their steps through the tunnel; Tristan knew they were approaching Rajesh long before he came in sight, because his ragged, panicked breathing filled the tunnel.

"You okay?" Ori asked brightly when he spotted Rajesh.

Rajesh glared at him. "Let's get the hell out of here."

Though he said nothing, Tristan had to admit it was a relief when he reached the top of the rope and flopped back onto the rocky floor of the main cave. The weight in his chest eased slightly, and somehow the gloom seemed less overpowering.

That night, they debated their options with more intensity than before. Ilana would arrive any day now, and still they lacked a true plan. Amber argued that she would be able to find her way through the underground labyrinth without trouble, but Rajesh refused to go down the shaft again until they had a proper rope to guide their way.

"There has to be something we can use," Pavlina insisted.

While they talked, she sorted through the piles of clothing the other students had left behind. It wasn't until hours later that Tristan realized what she had been doing—as he handed her a cup of soggy pasta, he spotted a pile of bent-up yarn beside her and a single piece of fabric on her lap. She'd been unwinding someone's sweater so they could use the string to mark their way.

"Rajesh!" Tristan beckoned him over. "Look at this! You ready to find a way out tomorrow?"

Spotting the messy pile of yarn that Pavlina was just beginning to wind into a ball, Rajesh shook his head. "You win. I'll do it."

Tristan grinned. "Thanks, Pavlina."

She gave him a half-smile as if to say, "I told you so."

"What are we going to do if we find a way out?" Rajesh asked.

"We have to figure out some way to ambush Ilana when she arrives," Tristan said. "I have no idea how. Hopefully she'll be distracted with the barrier, so we'll be able to get close enough to destroy that globe."

"How will we do that?"

"Throw a sack full of marbles at the globe, with a lit match and a fuel canister," Ori suggested from the other side of the cavern.

Tristan nodded. "That's probably our best chance. Then we run like mad."

"What happens afterwards?" Rajesh asked. "Can we come with you? Or would your headmaster kill us?"

"He wouldn't," Tristan said. "You have to come. If you want to, I mean.

"I will," Rajesh said. "I don't have anything else to go

back to."

"Same," Pavlina said.

They looked at Ori. He pretended to take great interest in his lumpy pasta. "I've got a family who still remembers me," he muttered. "I've never said a word, because I was scared Ilana would kill them off if she knew. I have to go home to them."

"You should," Tristan said. "You're very lucky to have them."

"Are you sure your headmaster won't hate us for what we've done?" Mei Ling asked. She sat against the far wall, hugging her knees with a mournful expression.

"Of course not," Tristan said. "We couldn't have managed any of this without you."

Rajesh cautiously approached Mei Ling. "You don't regret joining us, do you?"

She shook her head fiercely. "Never."

Tristan had hardly drifted off to sleep when he heard a commotion. Struggling to rouse himself, he reached for his headlamp and switched it on.

Someone yelled.

"What's going on?" Rajesh shouted.

Two voices were yelling now, and in the weak glow of his light, Tristan could make out a tangle of bodies locked in some sort of struggle.

One of the yells turned to a scream.

"Get off me!"

It was Ori.

Struggling out of his sleeping bag, Tristan bounded over to the wrestling pair. Only when he got closer did he recognize the second boy—Blake.

And he was holding a knife to Ori's throat.

"Leave us alone!" Tristan shouted. He reached in his pocket for a marble, but found none. Unable to summon up any magic, he hurtled into Blake and slammed his fists into the bigger boy's ribcage.

Blake twisted and threw Tristan off as easily as if he was swatting away a cat. He released Ori's neck in the process, though, and Ori took advantage of the opening to drag himself away.

"Traitor," Blake growled. Turning away from Tristan, he thrust his knife at Ori's thigh and sunk the blade in up to the hilt.

Ori howled in pain. As Tristan threw himself at Blake once more, Ori curled his leg to his chest, tears spilling from his eyes.

Rajesh came barreling into Blake just then, and for the first time he was overpowered. He crashed onto his side, but he recovered quickly.

"You'll pay for this," he yelled, jumping to his feet and facing down Tristan and Rajesh. As he raised his bloodied knife and lunged for Tristan, something moved in the shadows.

With a short gasp, Blake toppled to his knees. His eyes bulged, and he seemed to be struggling for air.

Amber stepped into the light cast by Tristan's headlamp, watching Blake with regret.

"You had to be stopped," she said softly.

With a final convulsion, Blake grew still.

"You killed him," Rajesh said in awe.

Tristan studied Amber for a long time; when she noticed, she gave him a small, grim nod. She would not retreat into herself again. The time for that was over.

No one remembered Ori until he choked out another sob and rolled onto his side.

"Ori!" Pavlina ran to his side. "Ori, are you okay?"

The others crowded around him, Blake already forgotten. Blood was pooling beneath his legs, dripping from between his fingers where he had clamped them over the deep wound.

"Amber," Tristan said in a low voice. "Can you help him?" He didn't want to get their hopes up if she couldn't.

"I can try. This is—worse than anything I've healed before, though."

Kneeling smoothly beside Ori, heedless of the blood that was now soaking into her pants, Amber lifted his hands aside and touched the skin that showed beneath his torn jeans. Though Ori howled in pain, he held himself motionless while Amber examined the wound.

"Can you give me a bit more power?" she asked Tristan. "I don't have enough to draw on down here."

He didn't have time to fetch a marble this time. Ori's face had gone pale and his heartbeat ragged. Grabbing Amber's hand, he reached deep into himself, shutting out everything until he thought he could feel the well of power waiting to be called upon. He drew on as much of it as he dared and sent it spiraling towards Amber, whose skin gave a jolt like static electricity as she received the power.

Tristan could hardly believe it had worked.

All four of them waited, motionless, as Amber bent her head over Ori's wound. For the longest time, nothing happened. The only sound came from a steady drip of water pattering onto the stone floor.

At last, Amber slumped back, her already white face completely drained of color.

"Will he be okay?" Mei Ling asked nervously.

"I don't know," Amber said. "I'm sorry."

Pavlina handed Tristan a sock, which he wetted and used to sponge blood away from the wound. Ori didn't flinch this time; he had lost consciousness. As the blood cleared, Tristan thought he could see a line of raw, barely-healed skin beneath. The scar was pink and angry-looking, but at least Ori was no longer bleeding.

"It looks like he's going to recover," Tristan said, dabbing away the last of the blood and tossing the filthy sock aside.

"If he hasn't lost too much blood," Rajesh said. "I guess we just have to wait until he wakes up."

"I healed the skin," Amber said, "but the knife cut right through his muscles. Those I couldn't fix. Not here. He might not walk again for a long time."

Pavlina's eyes widened in horror. "But Ilana's about to return!"

"We'll wait until morning to decide what we do," Tristan said heavily. "Hopefully he'll be awake by then."

While Tristan and Amber went off to rinse their hands with a discarded water bottle, Pavlina shifted Ori's head onto a pillow and nudged him gently onto a sleeping mat. Then she unzipped a sleeping bag and tucked it around his still form.

"Should we do something about him?" Rajesh asked, jerking a thumb back at Blake's lifeless body.

"He'll be fine here," Tristan said coolly. "They'll see him if we drag him anywhere else, and they'll probably blow this place up if they find out what we've done."

"Maybe," Rajesh said. "I don't think Ilana loved Blake as much as he thought she did."

Tristan didn't sleep at all that night. Despite his feigned nonchalance, he was uneasy with the thought that they were sharing the room with a dead body. He kept imagining he saw shapes moving around the room—Blake's ghost, or even Ori's—and had to turn on his headlamp twice inside his sleeping bag to remind himself what was real.

He woke with a pounding headache to find that Rajesh and Pavlina were already awake and tending to Ori. Rubbing his eyes, he joined them by the mountain of canned food. Ori was awake, propped against four sleeping bags in their stuff-sacks, and he had regained his normal color.

"Rajesh says you and Amber saved me," he said, smiling wanly as Tristan took a seat beside him.

"It was j-just Amber." Tristan yawned hugely. "How are you feeling?"

"Effing miserable. I can't move my leg—it hurts too

much." All of this was said in an incongruously light tone. "Look, Tristan. These guys won't listen to me, but I'm going to have to stay behind. I can't move, damn it! You're *not* allowed to just sit here with me and wait to die."

"You're not staying behind to die, either," Rajesh said fiercely. "What about your family?"

Ori blanched, but he quickly smoothed his expression. "They think I'm dead anyway. They can cope with it."

The noise had roused Mei Ling and Amber, who stumbled over to join the others beside Ori. Amber had dark circles under her eyes, and her face was still drained of color—clearly she had pushed herself harder than she would admit.

And it still wouldn't be enough.

Tristan wondered if it would have been kinder to let Ori bleed out on the cavern floor. He was likely to die no matter what they did, but at least that way it would have been a horrible accident rather than the result of someone's decision.

"You're not doing very well, are you?" Amber asked softly as she took a seat beside Ori. Though he tried to brush her away, she untied the bandana he'd knotted around his leg and examined the puckered pink scar. "I healed the skin, but everything else is still broken. You might not be able to walk yet."

"It's fine," Ori said offhandedly. "What's a bit of mobility when I'm alive?"

"How long until he recovers?" Rajesh asked.

Amber didn't meet his eyes. "If I could get him

outside, I could finish the job. But without help, he will take weeks to heal."

Ori sat up straighter than before and tugged his jeans down so the wound was no longer exposed beneath the hole Blake's knife had left behind. "Listen. You've got to leave me here. I'll be *fine*."

"And what happens when the teachers get in?" Pavlina said coldly. "Are you just planning to smile at them and pretend we kidnapped you?"

"What happens if they blast their way in and we're all here?" Ori countered. "They won't even stop to ask questions. We're dead if they find us."

"Maybe we could carry you," Rajesh said.

"Don't be stupid. How are you going to get me down that pit? Or through any of the narrow bits? What if you have to climb something while you're down there?" Ori shook his head. "I'd rather be stuck here than down there."

Tristan folded his arms. "We can decide later. Right now we have to pack. Each of us should grab enough food to last the group two days, and then take as many marbles as you can carry. Don't forget your sleeping bags."

"What about tents?" Rajesh asked.

"I have a feeling we're going to be on the run as soon as Ilana gets back. Tents will be too hard to set up, and too obvious."

With great reluctance, the others left Ori's side and began packing. Tristan wished they would move faster; Pavlina seemed to be deliberately taking her time, perhaps hoping Ori would make a miraculous recovery in the extra minutes she was affording him.

At long last, Tristan and his four allies had snapped their bags closed and tied their shoelaces.

"Does anyone have a map?" Tristan asked, trying not to look at Ori.

"I found one in Tony's stuff," Rajesh said. "I'll show you once we're outside."

Tristan nodded.

"I don't want to leave him," Pavlina said, her backpack lying neglected at her feet.

"You'd better go," Ori snapped. "I'm going to start throwing rocks at you if you don't leave soon."

"Come on," Tristan said heavily. "We have to get out of here." Hoisting his backpack onto his shoulders, he leaned over and clasped Ori's hand one last time. Ori nodded, his expression closed-off.

Then, not waiting to see who followed, he turned and left the main cavern.

Amber joined him in the cave mouth immediately, and they both kept to the shadows so the students outside wouldn't catch sight of them. Five minutes passed with no sign of the others.

"If they don't come, we'll have to do this alone," Tristan said quietly.

"I know." Amber leaned against a large rock, resting her backpack on the stone. "I thought it would be this way all along."

"Why?"

She glanced back at the cave mouth. "I don't trust

people. No one is as good as their word."

"I trust them," Tristan said. "They're not betraying us if they stay behind. I don't blame them if they don't want to leave Ori for dead."

Just as he turned and started down the tunnel, flashlight still off so he wouldn't attract attention, he heard soft footsteps behind him.

Rajesh, Mei Ling, and Pavlina had emerged from the cave, backpacks on, faces lined with sorrow.

"I hardly even knew him before we came here," Rajesh said softly as he fell into step behind Tristan. "I never actually talked to anyone before this. But—losing someone, so soon after I started caring again…"

"I know," Tristan muttered. "It's the worst thing I could imagine."

He thought he could imagine how it felt. Leaving the Lair, knowing he would likely never see his friends again— it had hurt more than he could say.

Around another bend, Amber switched on her headlamp and the others followed suit. They were silent apart from the clanking of their overstuffed backpacks.

When they reached the pit, Tristan slid down the rope first. The others took turns tying their backpacks to the end of the rope and lowering them to the bottom, where Tristan undid the knots and stuffed the packs one at a time through the slot. Once the others had joined him, they squeezed through the slot and started along the narrow passageway. Though Rajesh moved stiffly, he didn't utter a word of complaint.

At the underground brook, Amber led the way forward, this time allowing the water to flood her shoes. Tristan followed reluctantly, bracing himself for the cold. It was chilly, but not numbingly so, and after a few steps he grew acclimated to the temperature.

Then, all at once, the ground dropped out beneath him.

"Damn it," he said under his breath, feeling for the ground past the shelf.

"Oh, no," Rajesh said. "I don't like the look of this."

Sinking up to his waist, Tristan finally touched solid rock. "We've come this far already. Do you want to go back?"

"No!" With a scowl, Rajesh followed, his face screwed up as the water rose to his hips. Poor Mei Ling had water up to her ribcage—her sleeping bag would be soaked. Of course, they didn't know what lay ahead. They might all be swimming before long.

Little by little, they made their way through the water, each breathing a sigh of relief as it began to recede.

"How much longer is this going to go for?" Rajesh asked darkly.

"Don't ask me," Tristan said. "I've never been this way before."

Around one corner, Tristan heard a sudden splash.

"What's that?" Pavlina said in alarm.

Tristan jumped at the sight of ten writhing forms like tiny snakes hovering just beneath the surface of the water.

"I think they're eels," Mei Ling said, bending forward

with interest.

Pavlina scrambled backwards onto a ledge safely out of the water. "What if they're poisonous?"

"I'm sure they're fine," Tristan said. He was already on edge without Rajesh and Pavlina making things worse. As he forged on past the eels, Pavlina and Rajesh climbed onto the side shelf and edged over the pool. One eel escaped the indentation in the rock where it had hovered and darted upstream, and Mei Ling giggled in surprise as it wriggled past her. He had never heard her laugh before.

It seemed that a lifetime passed in that narrow tunnel, the walls echoing with the sloshing of water. If Tristan hadn't been so worried about what would happen once they made their way out, he might have enjoyed the adventure; as it was, he couldn't tear his mind from Ilana and Stefan and poor Ori. He could no longer feel the cold of the water, though his body temperature was steadily dropping; he would start shivering before long.

Would Ilana be waiting for them outside? Surely Tony knew about most of the back entrances; had he betrayed them to Stefan?

At last, Tristan was shaken from his stupor when Amber said, "Look! Up ahead."

Squinting through the darkness, he thought he could make out the faintest white glow on the limestone ahead.

"Please tell me that's the end of this goddamn cave," Rajesh muttered, pushing past Tristan to see what lay ahead. A minute later, he gave a whoop. "I can see outside!"

"Not so loud," Tristan said, though he was just as excited. Trying to walk more quietly than before, he joined Rajesh just before the mouth of the cave. A clear brook ran from the darkness into the pale sunlight, fed by clumps of melting snow. Unfortunately, they were in a grassy bowl of a valley littered with rocky outcroppings, with no shelter to speak of. If anyone went looking for them, they would be spotted at once. Worse, he had no idea where they were in reference to the main entrance to the cave.

Rajesh didn't seem to care about the danger just then. Throwing his pack aside, he flopped onto a snow-free stretch of grass and closed his eyes. Pavlina sat gingerly on a rock and glanced back at the narrow opening into the cave.

"What now?" Mei Ling asked softly, kneeling beside the stream and dipping her hands in the cold water.

"We have to find everyone else, and then we have to figure out somewhere to hide," Tristan said.

"That's not going to be easy," Rajesh said, rubbing his eyes and yawning. "Remember how far below us that forest was? We'd have to hike half a day to get from the trees up to the cave."

"What if we go above the cave?" Mei Ling suggested.

Rajesh's eyes widened. "That's brilliant."

"Dangerous, though." Tristan sat on another rock and eased his pack off his aching shoulders. They were safe enough for now; as long as they found somewhere to stay for the night, they would be fine. "Ilana's going to have to come on a helicopter or something if she wants to get the globe up here."

"She won't be looking for us, though." Rajesh sat up and rummaged through his pack. "I bet we could dig a hole and hide in there if anyone came near." He held up a tan-colored tarp, close to the shade of the dry grasses all around. "We could put this over the top."

"Good idea. It's going to be really snowy up there, though," Tristan said.

"Remember Greenland?" Rajesh said in amusement. "We can deal with a bit of snow."

"Where are we going to stay tonight, then?" Tristan asked. "Maybe we should've brought the tents."

Rajesh shrugged. "We could start heading toward the cave, if you want. I think that's Mount Owen—" he pointed at a lumpy, low peak riddled with rocky bluffs "—which means the cave should be on the other side."

"How do you know?"

"I was looking at that map I told you about. There's only one flat valley leading up to Mt. Owen, and it's the same one we followed from the hut to the cave. All the other sides are really steep."

Now that Tristan thought about it, the valley did look vaguely familiar. They were on the opposite side, though, not following the same route they had originally taken to the Bulmer cave.

"Everyone agree with Rajesh?" Tristan asked.

Amber and Mei Ling nodded; Pavlina just gave him a cold stare. She obviously hadn't forgiven him for abandoning Ori. For once, though, he wasn't questioning his own decision—they'd had no other choice. If they had stayed behind, they would have died together. When he and Amber had agreed to Drakewell's mad scheme, they had been forced to accept that stopping Ilana was worth sacrificing a few lives, their own included.

He wasn't going to argue with Pavlina. She had chosen to follow him this far, and if she wanted to turn back now, that was her decision to make. He picked up his backpack again, grunting at the weight, and started across the broad valley toward the uneven face of Mount Owen. Rajesh and Amber fell into step beside him, Mei Ling just behind. When he glanced over his shoulder, he saw that Pavlina was following as well, her mouth set in a grim line.

As they picked their way around deep snowdrifts and past tussocks and oddly glossy alpine plants, Tristan marveled at the fact that, reluctant though they might have been, Rajesh, Pavlina, Mei Ling, and Ori had been brave enough to turn their backs on the only world they had truly known.

Closer to the mountain, the grass turned to bulging limestone edifices, their contours hidden beneath the snow.

"Hey—look at this!" Rajesh said, running ahead onto a plateau of stone. "We can sleep down there!"

The cans in Tristan's pack clanked as he raced up to see what Rajesh was talking about. Peering ahead, he recognized the same plateaus riddled with deep crevasses they had passed on their way to the cave, some too narrow to fit down, others as wide as the cavern they had just left.

"That's perfect!" Tristan said.

Breathing hard, Mei Ling caught up with them and dropped her pack. Her eyes widened as she saw the deep crevasses. Regaining her energy at once, she jumped across one of the chasms and ran lightly along a stone plateau. "This one is huge! We should spend the night here."

The crevasse she had found was wider at the bottom than the top, with a few chunks of rock that made a stairway of sorts down the far side. Mei Ling lowered herself to the bottom of the narrow canyon and looked around. It was big enough for them to lie lengthwise, and she beckoned them to join her as she wandered around the depths of the chasm.

Lowering their packs after her, Tristan, Rajesh, and Amber joined Mei Ling in the crevasse. Aside from the melting snow, which occasionally dripped on their heads, it was a perfectly cozy little hideaway.

"You coming?" Rajesh called to Pavlina.

"Yes," she said, stepping reluctantly over the lip of the hole.

They cooked dinner in a couple of the small camping pots Tristan had packed, and both he and Rajesh managed to burn their pasta.

"I was about to say 'I'm glad we're out of that miserable cave,'" Rajesh said, "but then I realized we're still pretty much in a cave, just with a bit more light. I wish we didn't have to hide underground all the time."

"You have to admit this is pretty cool, though," Tristan said.

Rajesh grinned. "True."

They were just sitting down to eat when something caught their attention. If Tristan wasn't mistaken, it was the thrum of a helicopter approaching their valley.

He, Rajesh, and Mei Ling raced each other to the top of the rock staircase, careful to keep their heads below the bluffs, where they watched as a helicopter soared over a ridge in a direct line toward their hideout. Something swung beneath the helicopter, chained into place—something dark and round.

It was the globe.

Ilana had returned.

Chapter 12

The Second Globe

"We're too late," Tristan said, stunned. "We'll never get there in time." The sun was already setting; even if he hadn't been about to collapse from exhaustion, he wouldn't be able walk through the night here. It was too dangerous, with crevasses and half-melted snow ready to trip them up at every step.

"She won't be able to get through the barrier yet," Rajesh said. "They're probably going to try blasting it apart before long, but they won't want to destroy the marbles in the cave. That would set them back several years."

"We have to get there by morning," Amber said unexpectedly. "Otherwise we lose our advantage."

Tristan groaned.

"We can sleep a few hours first," she said. "I doubt we're far from the cave."

"I'll wake the rest of you up in two hours," Pavlina said from the bottom of the crevasse. "I don't think I'll be able to sleep anyway."

"Thank you," Tristan said. He followed Rajesh and Mei Ling back to their makeshift camp. "I'm really sorry I dragged you into this," he told Pavlina in an undertone. "I had no idea Ori would—"

She shook her head fiercely, eyes glistening. "I'm glad. I've never felt so alive. Or so miserable. Before, we were just going through the motions. This is—" She trailed off, fingers digging into the limestone wall.

"How are we going to do this?" Rajesh asked from behind Tristan.

He turned. "We should do what Ori said—put all of our marbles into someone's backpack with a fuel can, light the whole thing on fire, and drop it over the globe. If it's conveniently sitting right in front of the cave, that is."

"That'll be really subtle," Rajesh said sarcastically. "Effective, though."

"That's all we need. Now get some sleep. We can't be collapsing halfway up the mountain."

Finishing the last of his charred pasta, Tristan followed his own advice, digging in his pack for his sleeping bag. Despite his bone-deep exhaustion, sleep didn't come easily. A steady rhythm like a ticking clock was running through his head, as though he was counting down the seconds until Ilana had destroyed the barrier. Ori wouldn't stand a chance—Tristan tried not to think of him lying in the cave alone, only the pile of marbles and Blake's dead body remaining for company. Each time this thought struck him, his legs itched to start running, to chase Ilana down before it was too late…

He lay restlessly and watched as the stars came out in the sliver of sky visible above their crevasse. The moon rose before long, dimming the stars and lending a silvery glow to the limestone. Every so often, a drip of water would plop onto his forehead, startling him back into alertness.

He had just drifted off into a troubled sleep when Pavlina rose and turned on her headlamp. "Time to go," she said. Though she had spoken softly, the others sat up almost at once. They had obviously been sleeping as uneasily as Tristan. They packed in silence, shrugging on extra layers and brushing condensation from their sleeping bags.

"You've all got your marbles handy?" Tristan asked, reaching into his bag to ensure that his stash remained near the top.

They nodded.

"Let's go, then."

In a quiet group, they climbed from the crevasse and started across the limestone bluffs. The snow had hardened in the cold night, and the moonlight reflecting off the white snowdrifts shed enough light to hike by. As they wove through the bluffs and along narrow strips of grass on their way up the mountain, Tristan couldn't stop thinking about Ori. He had justified abandoning him at the time, but now a knot of guilt had settled in his stomach.

The higher they climbed up Mt. Owen, the rockier the slopes grew, until only the occasional patch of grass emerged from among the solid mounds of stone. Tristan felt very exposed in the moonlight, though there were more than enough crevasses to jump into if they heard a helicopter approaching—provided they didn't break an ankle in the process.

The moon had sunk close to the peak of a nearby mountain by the time they reached the cairn that marked the top of Mount Owen.

"Any idea where we're supposed to go now?" Tristan asked Rajesh, dropping his pack and sitting on a rock.

"I think we just need to head down the southern side of the mountain," Rajesh said, digging in his pack.

"We should get everything ready now," Tristan said. "Let's fill one of our backpacks with all of the marbles and the fuel canister. Then we can leave the others behind when we get close to the cave."

"Just saying we survive, how are we supposed to get out of here?" Pavlina asked, opening her backpack and pulling out several handfuls of marbles.

With a rustle of paper, Rajesh produced a crumpled map from his pack. He unfolded it, revealing a large section of mountains labeled Kahurangi National Park. Mount Owen was near the center, and Tristan recognized Granity Pass Hut to the north of the peak.

After scrutinizing the map for a moment, Rajesh said, "That's the cave there. If we drop into the valley below it, we can link up with a road and follow it back out to the closest town."

"How long do you think that's going to take?" Tristan asked skeptically.

"Several hours." Rajesh traced the route a couple times before folding the map and slipping it into his back pocket. "And even when we get to the road, we'll probably be stranded in the middle of nowhere."

"New Zealand's not *that* big of a country, is it?" Tristan said. "We can probably walk to the next town. God, I wish we knew how to fly Ilana's helicopter. That would be a lot easier than walking."

Rajesh snorted. "Yeah. Where's a good pilot when you need one?"

Tristan ended up emptying his backpack to carry the marbles, while the others shared the rest of his supplies between them. His sleeping bag was too bulky to fit, so it got abandoned on the mountaintop along with two extra pairs of socks and one of the camping pots.

Cautiously now, they began picking their way down the southern face of Mt. Owen. The rocky slope was much steeper on this side, and several times they had to backtrack to circle around vertical bluffs. Before long, Tristan thought he recognized the grassy shelf surrounded by rocks where the cave entrance lay. His suspicions were confirmed when he spotted a tent pitched on a small patch of grass between two towering boulders.

"Leave your stuff here," he said quietly. "And make sure no one sees you."

"Hopefully everyone will be looking at the cave mouth," Amber said. "We can't exactly hide up here."

"Where's the helicopter gone?" Rajesh asked.

Mei Ling pointed at a glint of silver far below. "There."

She followed Pavlina's example and shoved her backpack under a rock lip, where it wouldn't be seen from overhead.

"That means it's dropped the globe somewhere," Tristan said slowly. "I...think this might actually work."

Hugging the rocks, they began creeping closer, on the lookout for anyone moving around outside.

Just as they were closing the final distance between the rocks and the top of the cave mouth, Tristan heard a voice.

"Ilana! Someone's up there!" It sounded like Stefan.

Cold with fear, Tristan dropped quickly behind the nearest rock. "Can you distract them?" he whispered urgently to Amber. This was not going well.

She nodded. "Be quick." While Tristan sheltered in the shadow of the rock, heart pounding so loud he couldn't concentrate on much else, Amber led Rajesh, Pavlina, and Mei Ling down the final grassy stretch beside the cave mouth toward the shelf.

Tristan couldn't see what was happening below, but he could hear tents being unzipped and canvas shifting. As soon as Amber and the others were out of sight, he wished he had gone in their place. Their job would be far more dangerous than his.

Shouts rose from the shelf below, and Ilana's voice cut through the clamor, saying, "You haven't fooled me, you idiots. Besides, you're too late. No matter what you do, I have already succeeded. The spell has been set."

Suddenly the shouts grew more urgent. Tristan pressed his back sharply into the rock, willing himself to stay put. He prayed it wasn't one of his friends who was shouting.

Yellow light rose from the rocky shelf—one of the tents had caught fire.

That would have been Amber's doing.

Hoping everyone's attention was fixed on the burning tent, Tristan crawled forward, unbuckling his pack as he went. He felt giddy with apprehension, his nerves on fire. He stopped just before the ledge and peeked over, lying flat on his stomach. To his intense relief, no one was looking his way.

There it was.

Just below, in a shallow indent on the grassy shelf, lay the globe. It looked a bit grimier than before, but otherwise unchanged.

It was easily within reach. Everyone below was looking at Amber, Rajesh, Mei Ling, and Pavlina; no one kept an eye on the globe. As long as Tristan managed to set the marbles properly alight, he should have no trouble. It was still dark, so he couldn't make out faces, but he could hear Ilana and Stefan shouting at Amber.

Fumbling with one of the six marbles in his pocket, Tristan set his pack down on the ledge and concentrated on a flame. It was almost too easy—with his nerves racing, the fire sprang to his fingertips almost by accident. The backpack took a moment to catch, and when a stiff breeze raked through his hair, he held his breath, worried it would go out. The flame died for a moment, fading to a stream of smoke, and then it leapt to life again. Tristan exhaled heavily, trying not to panic.

The gas canister was buried deep within his backpack.

When should he throw the pack? If he did it too soon, everyone would hear, and they would move it away from the globe at once. But if he waited too long, the whole mass would explode in his hands.

Before he could make up his mind, the decision was made for him. The flame leapt high in the air before him, nearly singeing his chin.

"What's that?" a girl's voice called from below.

Tristan swore. He had been seen.

There was no time to lose. Both arms around the pack, face averted from the flame, he took aim and hurled it at the globe.

It fell short, landing two paces before the globe.

"Get that away from here!" Ilana yelled from the opposite side of the group. Amber, Rajesh, Mei Ling, and Pavlina were forgotten as Ilana and her followers crowded around the globe to see what was happening. "No, you idiots!" Ilana shouted. "Stand back!"

As the crowd below shuffled about in confusion, some moving closer to the globe while others tried to escape the melee, Tristan saw a bright white streak disappearing below the hillside.

Amber was safe.

There was nothing more he could do. Below, the backpack was burning merrily, sending up green and purple streaks of flame. Scrambling away from the ledge, Tristan edged down the slope to the shelf below, still breathing as though he had sprinted over Mount Owen. He couldn't see any of his friends, though he kept an eye on the spot where

Amber had disappeared.

As the blaze grew brighter than ever, most of the crowd backed away from the globe, sensing that something terrible was about to happen. A lone figure broke through the crowd and dashed towards the burning pack.

Stefan.

The teacher lifted the pack into his arms, yelping in pain as the fire washed over his face. Ilana came running after him, shouting, "Quick! It's going to—"

BOOM.

With a sound like a cannon, the pack exploded.

Tristan was thrown off his feet and into the rock behind him, where he lay for a long moment, dazed and off-balance. When he struggled to stand, wincing at the bruise between his shoulder blades, he saw nothing but chaos below.

At first he couldn't even recognize the grassy shelf. Was he dreaming?

Instead of an enormous globe below, there was nothing but a deep hole gouged in the rock. But as the smell of charred plastic and stove fuel rose to meet him, he realized that the entire rocky shelf had been obliterated.

Ilana's globe was gone.

Head spinning, Tristan started down the hillside once more, eyes out for Rajesh, Mei Ling, and Pavlina. He couldn't find them in the crowd.

No one noticed him. Ilana was nowhere to be seen, and students were scattering in every direction.

Hoping the others could take care of themselves, he

darted in the direction that Amber had disappeared. In the darkness, no one picked him out of the crowd.

There—just over the hillside, half-hidden behind a rocky outcropping, Amber waited for him. It was a good thing she had run when she did—her silver hair stood out like a beacon in the moonlight.

"Tristan!" Amber called softly. "Where are the others?"

"You didn't see them?" He ducked behind the rock that hid her and crouched down.

Amber shook her head. "We all ran when you threw the pack. I didn't see them afterwards."

"I guess we just have to wait," Tristan said tensely. Blood was coursing through his veins; he wanted nothing more than to start running and never look back.

A few shapes came barreling down the hillside on either side of them, and Tristan quickly yanked his black wool hat over Amber's white hair. She understood at once and began stuffing the ends of her hair beneath the hat. Still no one saw them.

They still had a chance of getting away safely.

From their hiding place, Tristan carefully watched each figure that appeared on the hillside, searching for his friends. At long last, a dark-faced figure with another shape in its arms staggered down the slope.

Rajesh was carrying Mei Ling, who was barely stirring. Tristan waved him over, and Rajesh nearly collapsed when he deposited Mei Ling on the grass behind Amber.

"Where's Pavlina?" Tristan asked quickly.

"She ran the wrong way. I think she's gone after Ori."

Tristan cursed. "We don't have time for that!"

"I…don't think she'd want us to follow her," Rajesh said slowly.

Tristan groaned. He had dragged Pavlina into this mess in the first place, and he felt responsible for getting her out alive.

"I think you got Ilana and Stefan, though," Rajesh said. "That'll help things."

"There are still too many of them," Tristan said. "We're screwed."

"We have to leave now," Amber said softly. "Pavlina made her decision when she turned back."

Tristan opened his mouth to argue, but Rajesh said, "Come on. We have to get out of here." Taking a deep breath, he lifted Mei Ling once more and started down the hill, walking with the staggering gait of a drunkard.

Just as they reached the start of a steep scree slope, a voice bellowed at them from behind.

"*They're escaping!*" It was Mordechai.

Tristan went cold as he looked over his shoulder and saw Mordechai and three other burly figures starting down the hill.

"We have to hurry," Amber said quietly. "Drakewell needs to know about the spell Ilana set."

"Rajesh can't go any faster," Tristan said tensely.

"Leave us behind," Rajesh said. "They probably won't hurt us."

"Of course they will," Tristan snapped. "Don't be

stupid."

Mordechai was gaining on them quickly. Rajesh was barely making progress down the scree slope, stepping carefully as the ground shifted underfoot.

"Amber. You go on ahead." Tristan stopped and gave her a flat stare. "You'll make it out alive. Go and warn Drakewell, and make sure no one follows you. I'll stay and help Rajesh."

"You'll bloody well die!" Rajesh said in alarm.

"I won't just abandon you," Tristan said. "I've already abandoned too many of my friends."

Amber froze, eyes on the approaching figures. "I can't—"

Tristan grabbed her wrist. "Go. Get out of here!"

After a long pause, she tore her gaze from Mordechai and stumbled down the slope. She made quick progress on her own, and had vanished into the beech forest at the foot of the mountain within minutes.

"You're an idiot," Rajesh mumbled, though he continued picking his way down the slope with the same dogged determination.

"Can I help carry her?" Tristan asked, one eye on the approaching figures. They were close enough now that he recognized Ricardo and two enormous students from the Second Division whose names he had never bothered to learn.

"I'm fine," Rajesh grunted.

They were approaching the bottom of the scree slope—Tristan dared to hope that they might shake

Mordechai off in the woods.

"Stop right there!" Mordechai shouted after them. "What've you done with the albino?"

"She's gone," Tristan yelled over his shoulder. "You're too late!"

Something slammed him in the small of the back, knocking his feet out from under him. He landed on his tailbone, yelping in pain, and looked around wildly to see what had hit him.

Ricardo was laughing nastily. A large, flat rock lay just behind Tristan, and as he watched, Ricardo lifted another rock and sent it after Rajesh. He had to be enchanting the rocks, because no one could throw that far.

"Duck!" Tristan yelled as the second rock hurtled towards Rajesh's head.

Rajesh dropped to his knees just in time to avoid a nasty concussion.

Struggling to regain his feet, Tristan turned to face Mordechai. It was too late to run. He, Rajesh, and Mei Ling could do nothing but give Amber a head start.

"Why did you stay behind?" Rajesh groaned, setting Mei Ling down on a grassy patch and staggering a few paces away from her.

"I couldn't leave," Tristan said harshly. "I just couldn't."

Rajesh coughed. "Well, you're an idiot. Let's get away from Mei Ling. I don't want them noticing her."

"I think we're a bit late for that," Tristan muttered, though he stumbled away from her stirring form.

Mordechai and his cronies were closing in.

Behind the distant horizon, the first grey light of dawn was beginning to emerge. In the pale glow, Mordechai's face was thrown into hazy relief. His eyes were wild, his grin crazed.

"I smelled you for a traitor the first time I ever saw you," he spat, reaching for another small boulder.

His three followers slowed as he did, their faces painted with matching expressions of bloodlust. These were the troubled students, the ones Mordechai had broken and bent to his will. If he hadn't escaped when he did, Landen would have become one of them someday.

They were Ilana's most devoted disciples.

"Don't let Tristan escape," Mordechai ordered, not bothering to keep his voice down. He stopped just a few paces above Tristan and Rajesh, caressing the boulder with his callused, tattooed hands. "Ilana should have given you to me from the start. She was too gentle with you."

"Ilana's dead," Tristan shot back, hoping it was true.

"Shame," Mordechai said softly. "Lucky she's got me to carry on in her stead."

He raised the boulder, and in a chilling instant Tristan realized his three followers had taken advantage of the distraction and armed themselves with rocks and knives.

Tristan went cold. Though he had meant to stand his ground, he found himself edging backwards. More than Ilana, more than any of her teachers, Mordechai terrified him.

Digging in his pocket, Tristan reached for a marble. He

only had three left—the rest had blown to pieces in his backpack.

"I see that marble," Mordechai said mockingly. "Not a very good magician, are you? Ilana told me you never mastered using your own strength for spells."

As Tristan tried to shut down his thoughts and focus on the marble, Mordechai aimed and hurled the boulder at his face.

Tristan threw himself to the side—

—and fell right into a short hole Mordechai had gouged into the grassy shelf. His ankle gave a horrible snap, and as he flung out a hand for balance, he dropped the marble.

Before he could straighten, a small flame sprang up in the grass and darted after him, quick as lightning.

He dodged out of the path of the flame, only to realize it was headed straight for Mei Ling.

"Leave her alone!" Rajesh bellowed, jumping over the line of fire to drag her out of the way.

Tristan groped in his pocket for another marble, trying to stamp out the approaching flame. This was something he could handle—back in Millersville, Alldusk had taught their class how to put out a fire in every way imaginable.

There it was. Clutching the marble in his numb hand, Tristan drew the power into him, eyes fixed on the fire. Then he released the magic from the marble into the air around him, summoning every drop of humidity and condensation to him until the ground beneath the fire was drenched.

As the air grew hazy with fog, the fire flickered lower and finally sizzled out.

Before he could straighten and face Mordechai once more, something slammed into his shoulder.

With a shout, Tristan whirled. Ricardo had circled around to the slope below him, and he was advancing on Tristan with a mocking grin.

"Rowan Drakewell's best students can't handle a few oafs throwing rocks," Ricardo taunted. "What if we had guns?" He reached for something in his pocket. "Oh, that's right. I forgot." He pulled out a small revolver and twirled it in his hands. "Say goodbye to Mei Ling."

With a wordless howl, Rajesh leapt at Ricardo.

Heart in his throat, Tristan dug for his last marble. Hazily he recalled the barrier spell he had learned the previous year, crouching in a hollow with sticks across the entrance.

The marble wasn't in his pocket.

It must have fallen out when he tripped.

To his right, Ricardo and Rajesh were wrestling on the ground, both grunting in pain as they rolled over the sharp rocks below. With a deafening *crack*, the revolver discharged. No one screamed, so it must have misfired.

"You thought you were so clever," Mordechai said, face lit up with a scornful smile. "You thought you could dupe us all."

At least Mordechai didn't have a gun. Tearing his eyes from the man's cruel face, Tristan realized that Ricardo had knocked Rajesh temporarily unconscious. As he raised the revolver once more, Tristan's hands grew hot with anger.

Boom! Something flashed bright white, and for a second Tristan thought Rajesh had been hit.

Then he saw that it was Ricardo, not Rajesh, who was howling and crawling backwards.

Tristan blinked in confusion. It took a moment before he recognized the power coursing beneath his skin and realized that he had inadvertently used magic—from where, he had no idea—to blow up the gun in Ricardo's hands.

Mordechai took advantage of Tristan's momentary distraction. As Tristan was turning back to face the teacher head-on, something struck him in the back so hard that he went sprawling.

His face smashed into a rock, and he felt something hot dribbling down his lip.

When he tried to roll over and struggle to his feet, a great pressure held him down. As he lay there, unable to move, a great volley of rocks came clattering free of the hillside and tumbled down to bury his legs. It was all he could do to bite his tongue and keep silent, blood pooling above his lip and trickling into his mouth with a bitter, rusty grit. It hurt so much he thought he would break into pieces.

From right behind him, Mordechai's voice whispered, "She should have let me break you. Such a gem you would've been. But it's too late. Ilana is gone, and you're going to die."

His knife was at Tristan's neck. But instead of slitting Tristan's throat and finishing the job, he turned the handle down and dug the point into his shoulder blade.

Tristan screamed. The pain was blinding him, sending a haze over his eyes. He prayed to lose consciousness.

Suddenly, Mordechai was thrown backwards. The great pressure on Tristan eased, and he was able to raise his head enough to see what had happened.

Amber was sprinting up the hill towards him.

Tristan could have cried in relief.

As Mordechai fumbled to stand, Amber dashed to Tristan's side and whispered, "I can't hold them off alone. Can you help? Use the forest."

He nodded, though he didn't know what he could do against four enormous magicians. He hardly knew how he would find the strength to stand.

Straightening, Amber strode forward, her hair silver in the pale light of dawn. She had lost her hat somewhere in the forest, and she stood out like a candle amidst the grey rocks.

As Tristan watched, frozen with anticipation, she summoned up a gust of wind that carried a thousand needles of ice. The wind slammed into Mordechai and his cronies, sending them all sprawling onto the rocks.

Tristan wiped his bloody nose on the back of his sleeve and scrambled to his feet. He couldn't afford to waste any more time.

Their only chance for safety lay in the trees a hundred feet below. Rajesh was already on his feet, bending over Mei Ling, who was sitting up and blinking around in confusion.

"Get to the woods," Tristan said under his breath.

Rajesh nodded without turning. Bending, he lifted Mei Ling into his arms once more and started down the hill, heavily favoring his left leg.

Though Tristan wanted nothing more than to stay and help Amber, he was virtually powerless without a marble to draw on. He started down the slope after Rajesh, watching Amber over his shoulder. As soon as the torrent of wind eased, the hillside began shifting, and a river of rocks started cascading down the slope. Mordechai and his followers scrambled to their feet, but they didn't quite make it before the rocks hit. One of the boys from the Second Division dodged to the side and managed to escape with nothing more than a rock in one leg, while the other two were dragged under, yelling and cursing.

For a moment, Tristan thought Amber had finished them off. But he should have known better.

With an explosion of shale, Mordechai tore himself free from the rockslide. Ricardo dug himself free soon after, and this time they turned on Amber without hesitation.

Rajesh and Mei Ling had nearly reached the safety of the trees.

Above, Amber took two hasty steps back, raising an arm as though summoning a new spell.

"See you later!" Tristan shouted. "I'll be telling Drakewell exactly where to find you!" He tried to imitate Mordechai's derisive tone, but he merely sounded angry.

It worked. Mordechai whirled at Tristan's voice and started downhill, quickly gaining momentum. He didn't appear to have been injured in Amber's rockslide.

Tristan cursed under his breath. Rajesh wasn't going to make it to the trees in time.

But Mordechai didn't seem to see Rajesh. He came pounding down the slope directly towards Tristan, who turned and ran for the trees as fast as he could. The deep gash in his shoulder was forgotten as adrenaline coursed through him.

Chapter 13

Out of the Woods

A s he ran, Tristan stretched his mind out, feeling for the aura of the forest ahead. The moment he passed beneath the trees, he could sense the magic hanging all around him like a web. He slowed, grabbing a tree to break his reckless momentum, and turned.

Mordechai had almost reached the trees. Behind him, Amber stood alone on the slope. The other three magicians must have fallen.

Reaching out tentatively, Tristan prodded at the network of magic hovering around him. Mordechai was only a few paces behind him, so he tentatively drew a small breath of power into him and sent it towards the outermost row of beech trees. Reverting to one of the first spells Alldusk had taught them during their stay in Millersville, he drew the trees' branches together and knotted them into a dense, springy wall.

The trees moved so quickly they could have simply been swaying in the breeze, and a second later Mordechai crashed into the wall of branches. The branches held, throwing the magician backwards. Swearing, Mordechai changed course and barreled around the wall.

Tristan had already turned and started running again, and as he passed over the decaying leaves, he reached out tendrils of magic towards the ground, coaxing any stray seedlings that lay beneath to grow. He didn't stop to see whether it was working—he could hear Mordechai's heavy footsteps behind him, punctuated by labored breathing.

In a sudden burst of light, a flame sprang up before him, too close to avoid. He ran right over the fire, scorching his leg, but he didn't have time to stop and see how bad the damage was. For an instant he wondered if he had accidentally sparked a fire in his over-use of magic; then he heard Mordechai laughing, and another flame leapt to life ahead of him.

He veered to the left, but the fire spread.

Glancing wildly over his shoulder, he saw Mordechai doubled over with laughter. The fire was closing in around him.

Skidding to a stop, Tristan reached into the soil and drew on the moisture collected there. Even before he could bring a layer of condensation to the surface, the fire began petering out. The ground was already so wet that the flame hadn't stood a chance.

Not waiting for the fire to go out, Tristan leapt over the smoldering remains and kept going.

Down another short slope and around a rocky outcropping he ran, blind with fear, hoping against hope that Amber was managing to hold the others off on her own. He continued urging plants to grow everywhere he ran, not stopping or looking back. The woods had grown quiet all around him, the first rays of sunlight just touching the treetops, and he began to wonder if he had thrown off his pursuers.

Behind a large boulder, he slowed and looked behind him. He could see no sign of movement, not even a breath of wind to stir the branches. In his path he had left a trail of saplings, some of them still growing visibly, others no taller than his ankle.

Just for good measure, he turned right and cut across the hill for several hundred feet. He couldn't hear Mordechai any longer, but he couldn't shake the feeling that he was still nearby.

When he paused, he discovered that he had gone much farther downhill than he'd realized. Looking across the valley below, the opposite hill now washed in golden light, he saw that he had descended almost to the foot of Mt. Owen. If the treeline was the same on every slope, he had a long way to climb before he reached the rocky meadow once more.

He should never have abandoned Amber and Rajesh. Anything could have happened in his absence.

Worried now, he turned and reassessed the hillside, trying to remember which path he had followed. The trail of saplings had ended before he cut to the right, so he had nothing to guide his way back.

As he began climbing, sweat trickled down his back,

and he stripped down to his shirt, draping his sweatshirt and down jacket over his shoulders. He didn't want to slow, but his breath rasped in his throat and his skin was beginning to boil. If only he had a drink of water...

Eventually he could continue no longer. He stopped, gasping, and leaned against a tree to catch his breath. His legs were on fire, and sweat had soaked his shirt. The pain in his shoulder was growing more insistent than ever, a deep, gnawing bite like a toothache. He was afraid to look at the damage, afraid that the moisture that soaked his back was more blood than sweat.

He had been so stupid. He should have stayed with the others. For all he knew, Mordechai could have turned back and finished his friends off while he was busy running for his life.

And now, he didn't even recognize where he was. The trees were thicker up ahead, the slope cluttered with fallen trunks, and he couldn't see far enough past the leaves to recognize the terrain before him.

The sun was fully up now, its light stark on the trees. As Tristan started uphill once again, this time moving slowly over the mess of undergrowth and half-rotted tree trunks, the certainty that he was lost settled on him.

For the first time since they had left the cave, true fear bit at him. Before, adrenaline had spurred him to keep moving, running, pressing on. Now, he was filled with a growing panic. What if he never found the others again? If only he had another marble for an Intralocation spell.

There was nothing to do but keep moving uphill.

Almost sick with worry now, he forged on, the dull ache in his shoulder strengthening with a vengeance.

As he went, the slope grew steeper and steeper, parts of it giving way to former rockslides and sheer rock faces.

When he reached the aftermath of yet another mudslide littered with rocks and unearthed roots, the foot of the slope piled with dead trees, he turned to the right and cut across the hill, hoping he could find a stretch of forest that he recognized.

That turned out to be a worse plan than before. Soon he stumbled across a vertical stretch of hillside that he could see no way around. Cursing under his breath, he continued across the hill to the right, certain he had already passed the section of forest he had initially come through.

Suddenly, the leaves rustled above him. He froze, grasping for the magic of the forest. As usual, it eluded him.

A second later, Rajesh crashed through the trees, Mei Ling in his arms. He was pale, his face screwed up in pain, but he was still blessedly alive. Amber followed a moment later, moving silently over the dead leaves.

Tristan nearly collapsed in relief.

"How the hell did you guys find me?"

"Intralocation spell," Amber said. "You weren't that far away, though I was afraid we would never get to you. We nearly ran over a cliff!"

"Sorry," Tristan said. "I got completely lost. And I used up all of my marbles on Mordechai."

"What now?" Rajesh asked, setting Mei Ling down and shaking out his arms. "I can't keep going like this much longer."

"Let me have a turn carrying her," Tristan said. "It's going to be a long way. We have to get out of here and find the nearest airport."

"How are we going to afford plane tickets?" Amber asked. "We no longer have our passports, either."

Rajesh reached in the pockets of his enormous coat and pulled out a handful of Euros, two credit cards, and their passports. "I raided as much as I could find while we were packing. I've got Pavlina's passport, too. I hope she'll be okay without it."

"I just hope she's still alive," Tristan said darkly. "I'm sure she can figure out a new passport."

"Which way?" Rajesh asked.

"Left," Tristan said. "It's completely vertical to the right. We'll make it down to the river, and then figure out what to do from there. Does anyone have some water? I'm dying."

Rajesh tossed his water bottle over. "Careful—we're rationing. I had to dump Mei Ling's backpack near the cave."

Tristan gulped at the icy water. He could have finished off the whole bottle himself, but he forced himself to pass it back to Rajesh.

"You sure you'll be okay with her?" Rajesh asked as Tristan lifted Mei Ling carefully into his arms.

"I'm not *that* weak," Tristan said, though his shoulder protested sharply at the weight.

When he turned, he heard a sharp intake of breath

from Amber. "What did you do to your back?"

"It's not that bad," Tristan insisted, though he felt a bit dizzy.

"Here, I can stop the bleeding," Amber said. She put a hand over his shoulder blade—he flinched at her touch, though it was lighter than a dragonfly's wing—and sent something warm spilling over his skin like sunlight. The sharp agony dulled to a persistent ache, and Tristan was able to straighten without gasping. He gave her a fleeting smile.

"You should give Mei Ling back to me," Rajesh said with concern.

"No, I'm fine!"

After about five steps, though, he had to admit that it was much harder than it looked to negotiate the tangle of downed trees and scrubby bushes with a heavy weight in his arms. Mei Ling was stirring, her lips twitching every so often; if they were lucky, she would wake before they reached the bottom of the slope.

"What happened to the others?" Tristan asked, stopping to catch his breath. At least he was no longer feeling so lightheaded.

"Amber buried them under a rockslide," Rajesh said. "When they tried to get up, she sent a giant root over them. They're not getting out any time soon."

Tristan glanced at Amber, who gave him a pointed look. He had a funny feeling that she could have killed them in the space of a heartbeat; it had been her reluctance to do any lasting damage that had delayed her.

At long last, they reached the foot of the hill, where they found a narrow stream. Though the air was icy, they found themselves stepping in the water several times to avoid steep sections of the bank. Tristan's shoes quickly filled with water, and before long he couldn't feel his toes.

Soon after they reached the stream, Tristan handed Mei Ling back to Rajesh, who murmured something in her ear as he lifted her into his arms. Tristan took Rajesh's backpack, feeling so weightless he could almost fly.

It was as they neared the end of the valley that Mei Ling opened her eyes at last.

"We got away?" she asked weakly.

Rajesh stopped so abruptly Tristan nearly walked into him. They were still wading through the stream, almost knee-deep in a section of gentle rapids. "Mei! Are you okay?"

"I think so," she said. "Where are we?"

Once he had passed the rapids, Rajesh set her gently on the bank and clambered onto a rock across from her. "We're nearly to the road, I think. If we're in the right valley, anyway."

Tristan forged on ahead and climbed onto a muddy stretch of the stream's bank, giving his icy feet a chance to thaw.

"Have you carried me this entire way?" Mei Ling asked wryly, rubbing her eyes.

"I wasn't about to leave you behind."

She gave Rajesh a fleeting smile. "I can walk now. I'll be okay."

"I'm not sure you should," Rajesh said at once. "You've had a bad concussion. I think you're supposed to lie down for the next couple days."

"Spare me the prognosis," Mei Ling said. "Let's just worry about staying alive for now."

Reaching for a tree branch, she pulled herself shakily to her feet. "I'm fine. See?" It was only after Rajesh turned away that she brought a hand to her head and prodded at what must have been a nasty bruise beneath her hair.

Tristan took the lead now, Rajesh in the rear so he could keep a careful eye on Mei Ling. Their progress was much faster now that she could walk, and before long they reached the bend in the valley. Around the base of this hill, the valley widened and their stream fed into a wide, shallow river.

It was not long after that when the trees thinned and then disappeared altogether. They had reached a stretch of dry, weedy pastureland. Tristan dropped the pack he was carrying and ran up a nearby hill, hoping against hope that he would find some sign of civilization in the distance—a town, perhaps, or even a lone settlement.

As he crested the top of the hill, he caught sight of a dilapidated barn, and beyond it, a road.

"There's the road!" he shouted down to the others.

"Thank god," Rajesh moaned.

As Tristan turned and picked his way back down the grassy hill, Rajesh dug in his backpack and unearthed their map.

"It's just that way," he told Tristan, waving the map to

his right. "It's five kilometers to a square, so…about eight kilometers to the next road. Maybe someone will be driving along that one." He frowned. "Do you have something else to wear? Your shirt's completely covered in blood."

Tristan tugged off his shirt, grateful when the barely-healed wound gave only a slight twinge of protest, and pulled on his sweatshirt instead. Amber wiped a spot of blood from his chin with her thumb, and he gave her a grateful smile.

They had only been walking for what felt like another hour when the hum of an engine rose in the distance.

"Someone's coming!" Tristan said. They all jumped off the road, Tristan holding up a thumb and the others following his lead.

Before long, the car roared around the bend—it was a truck, its bed piled with cuttings of some yellow-flowered plant. When the driver showed no signs of slowing, Rajesh jumped in front of it and waved his arms wildly.

The driver swerved to avoid him, shouting a curse out the window, but it worked—he slowed and came to a stop in the middle of the road.

"Oi! What're you doing?"

"We need a ride back into town," Tristan said hurriedly. "We were out backpacking, and my friend fell and got a concussion. We're trying to get back to Nelson so we can take her to the doctor."

The driver muttered something under his breath that sounded like, "Bloody tourists." Raising his voice, he said, "What've you done with your parents?"

"We're all eighteen," Tristan lied. "We came out hiking on our own."

"Well, I haven't got room in the front," the man said, "but you can sit in the bed. Careful, though—the gorse is sharp."

While the others piled into the back, Tristan climbed into the front seat.

"What are you doing out here?" Tristan asked, trying to distract the driver from asking any further questions.

"It's my job, mate." He revved up his truck with a sputtering roar. "Department of Conservation. Just back from a gorse-clearing mission."

"Oh." Tristan wished one of the others had taken the front seat. "Have you—uh—always worked here?"

"Twenty years this December."

An awkward silence fell, and after a pause the driver glanced at Tristan and said, "Not to pry, but what the hell were a bunch of kids doing out here in the goddamn middle of winter?"

"We were fine until M—until my friend fell. It's not very snowy up on the mountain."

The driver shook his head, though thankfully he subsided into silence after that. Every now and then he would mutter something under his breath, not looking at Tristan.

Nearly an hour passed before the bumpy road smoothed into pavement. Tristan hoped Mei Ling was doing all right; surely all this jostling couldn't be good for her. He didn't even want to imagine what would have happened if this truck hadn't driven along and found them at exactly the right time.

"It's another hour to Nelson," the driver said as they turned onto another road, this one wider than the last. "It's not on my way, but I can't just leave you out here. 'Specially not if that girl's got a concussion."

"Thank you," Tristan said quickly. "We really appreciate it."

At long last, they came to the outskirts of Nelson. The driver pulled up outside a medical center and said, "You'll call your parents now, right?"

"Of course," Tristan said. "Thank you so much."

They all climbed out of the car, Rajesh supporting Mei Ling, and the driver gave Tristan a long look before he drove away.

"He wasn't very nice," Tristan said.

"He gave us a ride," Rajesh said. "He might've saved us. I don't care if he was nice or not."

"Good point."

Since they had the money for it, and since Mei Ling was dangerously pale, they headed into the clinic and asked if someone could have a look at her.

"Have you been here before?" the receptionist asked.

"We're just traveling through," Tristan said. "Our parents are away for the day, and she's fallen off her bike and gotten a concussion."

To his relief, the receptionist didn't ask any more questions. Mei Ling was whisked off to another room while Tristan, Amber, and Rajesh sank into plastic chairs in the waiting room.

Chapter 14

Mordechai's Revenge

An hour passed, the hands on the clock moving so slowly Tristan almost thought they had stopped. He couldn't keep from glancing at the window every few minutes, expecting Mordechai and his cronies to appear around the corner. They couldn't possibly know where Tristan had gone, yet he still couldn't shake the fear.

At long last, Mei Ling reappeared, some of her color returned to her cheeks.

"She's not disoriented," the nurse said, "but you really should let her lie down. Keep a close eye on her for the rest of the day. If she sounds the least bit confused, don't let her fall asleep. I would have kept her, but she says you have a flight to catch later today."

"Yeah," Tristan said quickly. "How do we get to the airport from here?"

The receptionist called a taxi for them, and all four of them piled into the stuffy interior. Sitting on the clean leather seats, Tristan realized for the first time how filthy they must look. He hadn't seen his reflection in months now; his face and hair were probably caked with dirt and who knew what else.

Thankfully, the taxi driver didn't say a word, and they were dropped off at the small Nelson Airport in no time.

They were in luck. Since it was winter, none of the flights were crowded, and with the credit cards and Euros Rajesh had stolen, they were able to find seats on a plane to Auckland. From there, they would board a direct flight to Vancouver.

"What happens when we get to Canada?" Rajesh asked under his breath as they waited in line to board their first plane.

"I'm planning to figure that out when we get there," Tristan said. "As long as we're far away from Ilana's followers, we'll be fine."

Rajesh nodded grimly. Tristan wondered what lies he had been fed over the years regarding Drakewell and the Lair. For Rajesh and Mei Ling, defecting to Drakewell's side was just as daring as joining Ilana had been for Tristan and Amber.

Just before they reached the ramp, tickets in hand, an announcement came over the loudspeaker. "Rajesh Bhatia. Please report to the information desk immediately. Rajesh Bhatia."

Tristan went cold. "They've found us."

"Who is it?" Mei Ling whispered.

"Mordechai," Tristan said. "I'd bet my life on it. It sounds like the other three were pretty beat up when

Amber left them."

"What happened?" Mei Ling asked. "I don't remember anything after the globe exploded."

When Rajesh handed over his ticket, the man at the counter said, "Did you hear the announcement, young man?"

"It's just my aunt," he said dismissively. "She wanted to make sure I didn't forget the sweater she knitted me. But I left it behind on purpose."

The man chuckled. "Poor lady. Have a good flight."

"Quick thinking," Tristan said under his breath as he hurried to join Rajesh on the tarmac.

"You've got to be a good liar if you want to keep your head around Ilana."

"Go on," Mei Ling prodded. "What happened to Ilana?"

"I think she's dead," Rajesh said slowly. "I bloody well hope she is. Stefan, too. After the globe blew up, we set off running…"

Tristan started up the stairs onto the plane, a cold wind ruffling his hair, as Rajesh filled Mei Ling in on the whole miserable time.

"Where's Pavlina?" she asked.

Tristan turned to her with a grimace. "She went back for Ori. I have no idea what happened to her."

Mei Ling's eyes widened. "Poor Pavlina!"

The first flight passed quickly, and in Auckland they stopped for an enormous meal, all four of them ravenous, before boarding the international flight. The whole time Tristan kept waiting for an announcer to call out his name, but the loudspeakers remained silent. Mordechai must have lost their trail in Nelson.

As soon as the plane took off, Tristan fell fast asleep, stretched across all three of the empty seats in his row. He didn't wake up until many hours later, when the pilot announced that they were beginning their descent.

They made it through customs easily enough—Rajesh remarked that it was lucky they weren't flying into the US—and found an information desk to ask for a hotel. While the others looked around one of the Canadian-themed gift shops, Tristan bought a postcard shaped like a maple leaf and scrawled,

We'll be waiting at the Vancouver Bay Hotel. We've done it.

He didn't sign the postcard, because he was worried Mordechai might intercept it, and after asking a bored-looking information desk worker to look it up, he addressed it to the Millersville post office.

On their way out of the airport, he dropped the postcard into a mailbox, praying that the Canadian post was efficient.

They caught a taxi to the Vancouver Bay Hotel, where they checked into a room on the tenth story and settled in to wait. It was dark out, but the air was warm and heavy with humidity. It took Tristan a moment to remember that it was still summer here.

"I need a shower," Mei Ling said. "I'm filthy."

"We all are," Rajesh said. "I bet we reek!" He gave her

a sideways look. "You don't think you'll pass out, do you?"

"I would have done it already if I was planning to," she said. "I'll be quick. Don't worry."

As Rajesh and Amber unpacked their backpacks, throwing all of their dirty clothes in a heap in the corner, Tristan sat by the window and flipped through a binder filled with information on Vancouver, not paying any attention to the brochures within.

"I'm sorry I didn't kill him," Amber said in a small voice just behind Tristan.

With a start, he turned. Rajesh had left the room, and he was alone with Amber for the first time in weeks.

"Mordechai," she said. "I wish I had killed him."

"I was the one running away from him, not you," he said bitterly. "It's my own damn fault I wasn't quick enough."

"I still could have done it," Amber whispered. "But after Blake, I couldn't—" She looked down at her hands, turning them over to examine her palms. "What am I becoming, Tristan?"

"We've all changed," he said flatly. "You're not any worse than me. I would've killed them all if I was strong enough." He reached for her hand, but at that moment Rajesh returned with a pile of towels.

"I thought we'd need a few more of these," he said, throwing them onto the bed.

Amber sat down quickly, and Tristan turned back to the binder, Mordechai's face still haunting him.

It seemed that Mordechai had genuinely lost their trail

in Nelson, though. And now that they were here, so close to the Lair and yet still hundreds of miles away, thoughts of his friends were starting to push his fear of Ilana's magicians aside.

He wondered if things had changed in the Subroom in his and Amber's absence these past four months, or if life had gone on as before. Had they gone home for the summer, or had Drakewell held them back so Ilana wouldn't be able to target them?

The Lair invaded his head at night—once he dreamed that he returned to school, and no one could see him; several other times he dreamed that life returned to normal, and when he woke up he was disoriented to find that he wasn't nestled in the safe confines of the Subroom.

Four days passed. They washed every scrap of clothing they owned, wearing bathrobes as they waited for the laundry to finish, and threw out some of their fouler camping gear. They ate out for every meal until their money began to run low, and began discussing the feasibility of hitchhiking to Alberta and finding Millersville on their own. They spent their days wandering around Vancouver, exploring the waterfront and the parks. Tristan had a feeling they were all itching to get away from civilization.

Tristan wanted nothing more than to spend time with Amber, but she disappeared most mornings before he was awake, not returning until late at night. Though she was quieter than usual, he was relieved that she hadn't closed herself off like she had the year before. Whatever she had done to Ricardo and the other magicians, it hadn't messed with her mind.

Rajesh and Mei Ling wandered off together for three days in a row, and once Tristan caught them holding hands, though they both pretended nothing had happened when they returned that evening.

More often than not, Tristan was left to his own devices, exploring as much of the city as he dared without getting lost. He poked his head into museums, wandered through tree-lined parks, and sat on the pier watching little sailboats bobbing in the wake of larger ships.

One evening, he returned to the hotel before the others and did a double-take as he recognized a crowd of people waiting in the lobby.

Drakewell stood at the front, and directly behind him was Natasha. The students from the Subroom were clustered in one corner, some sitting against the wall, others gazing around the lobby as though they'd never seen a hotel before.

Tristan's heart swelled. He couldn't believe they were actually *here*, standing before him, after all this time.

It was a moment before anyone spotted him. Natasha said, "Tristan?" and suddenly everyone turned.

"Triss!" Leila cried out. She shoved Zeke out of the way and ran to Tristan, who hugged her tightly, laughing in relief. "I can't believe you're alive!"

"Me neither," he said wryly.

Leila released him, beaming, as the rest of the students from the Subroom took turns hugging him. Even Evvie gave him a brief hug, though Tristan couldn't remember what he had liked so much about her in the past.

"What the hell?" Eli said, grinning. "You shouldn't be here."

"What've you done with Amber?" Cailyn asked.

"She's fine," Tristan said, hugging Hayley and Trey in turn. "Just wandering."

Leila laughed. "No surprises there."

Even Natasha and Gracewright hugged Tristan once his friends were done, and Alldusk clapped him on the shoulder with a broad smile. Tristan avoided Alldusk's eyes, trying not to think of the terrible news he would have to pass on before long.

"Well," Drakewell said. "I assume your mission was successful?"

Tristan nodded. "We did what you asked us to. But we've got a lot to tell you. Ilana's done something terrible, and I don't know how we're going to stop it."

"Worse than building her own globe?" Drakewell asked sharply.

"I think so." Tristan glanced at the door, wishing the others were here to back him up. "She said it didn't matter what happened to the globe any longer, because she'd found a spell that would do more damage than the globe ever could."

Hayley gasped, and Eli cursed.

"You need to tell us everything," Natasha said hurriedly.

Tristan wanted Amber to be there—she knew more

about Ilana's spell than anyone. "Once the others get back, I'll tell you everything."

"Others?" Natasha raised an eyebrow.

"Two of Ilana's students escaped with us. There were supposed to be four, but the other two were—lost along the way. We never would've managed without them."

"We'll make a dinner reservation," Gracewright said briskly, "and you can give us the whole story then." She made for the reception and the phone waiting there.

"Wait," Tristan said, looking around the cluster of students and teachers. "Where's Delair?"

Drakewell's mouth tightened. "He never made it out."

"What d'you mean?" Tristan asked hurriedly, his excitement rapidly deflating. "What's happened?"

"There was an earthquake," Natasha said heavily. "We wondered if you and Amber had been involved, but—"

"No way!" Tristan said. "We haven't been near their globe in two months!"

"That's what I was saying," Natasha said. "The earthquake was on July twenty-first, which you couldn't possibly have mistaken for the tenth. We were starting to worry something had happened to you."

"So, Delair's—" He didn't want to say the words.

"Most of the Lair collapsed," Alldusk said. "We don't know how extensive the damage was."

Tristan winced. "But the rest of you are okay?"

"Damian's leg was broken quite thoroughly," Grindle-thorn said from the back of the group. He was almost entirely hidden behind Ryan's broad shoulders. "But he'll recover."

For the first time, Tristan noticed that Damian was leaning on a pair of crutches.

"Sorry," Tristan said.

"Like you care," Damian said sourly.

To his surprise, Tristan found that he did pity Damian. As obnoxious and uncaring as he could sometimes be, he was a hundred times better than Ilana and her disciples.

Just then, the automatic doors slid open to admit Rajesh and Mei Ling, both looking thoroughly ruffled from the stiff wind outside.

"Hey," Tristan called to Rajesh. "They're here."

Rajesh froze just inside the doors, eyes flickering warily from Drakewell to Natasha and back. Mei Ling continued forward, wide-eyed with curiosity. "So this is your school," she said, stopping beside Tristan.

He nodded. "Not very impressive next to Ilana's school, is it?" He turned. "This is Mei Ling. And that's Rajesh."

At last Rajesh started forward hesitantly. "Sorry. I know you don't want us here."

"Don't be silly," Natasha said briskly. "We're thrilled to have you."

Drakewell looked as though he didn't fully agree with her.

"We've got dinner reserved for seven o'clock," Grace-wright said, rejoining the group. "Am I correct to assume it's just Amber we're waiting on now?"

Tristan nodded.

As if on cue, Amber walked through the doors, stopping just as Rajesh had when she saw everyone from the Lair.

"Amber!" Leila called out. "We've missed you!"

As the rest of the group started towards the doors, Amber hunched her shoulders and submitted to being hugged by Leila, Rusty, Hayley, Cailyn, and Trey. Tristan caught her eye and grinned at her disarmed expression.

"I doubt you actually missed me," Amber told Leila under her breath as she followed Tristan into the windy night.

"No, we did," Leila said. "It's amazing how lonely it got with both you and Tristan away."

When Amber glanced skeptically at Tristan, he shook his head with amusement.

Gracewright had reserved the entire back room of a Chinese restaurant not far from the hotel, and it was only after they had ordered one of nearly every dish on the menu and the waitress had disappeared that Drakewell said, "Now. We are all impatient to hear what happened to you these past four months. Is the globe destroyed? And what should we expect from our enemies in the future?"

"It's a long story," Tristan said. "What's been happening on your end? We sent a ton of rain and a hailstorm on May tenth, but we haven't done anything since then."

"That rain flooded half of the Lair," Grindlethorn said sourly. "Don't you remember that hole the rogue magicians dug in the nearby cave? It still hasn't been patched."

Tristan grimaced. "Sorry. But what was that earthquake

you were talking about? And how did you figure out where Ilana was hiding in Greenland?"

"I think we should just start from the beginning," Natasha said. "You left, and life continued as normal for a while. We couldn't be certain you were alive until the tenth of May, when a flood and a hailstorm hit while we sheltered out in the woods."

"But everyone thought we just ran away?" Tristan asked.

"Everyone but Leila. She insisted some foul play must have been involved. After five days of listening to her list off the reasons why you and Amber would not have simply abandoned us, we drew her aside and told her the truth. We didn't want the others thinking too much about your absence."

Tristan glanced at Leila, who made a face. "I knew you wouldn't just *vanish*."

"Then, of course, Leila and Rusty insisted on searching for you on the globe. Leila spent every evening in the Map Room, until we started giving her regular shifts there. After nearly two months, she came running one morning to say she'd found a cluster of too-bright auras in Greenland.

"Quinsley tipped off the British newspapers, exposing an off-grid colony up in Greenland, and a week later we sent an earthquake after you. We wanted Ilana to know, without a doubt, that we had found her. We hoped she would flee, and in the confusion you would get a chance to destroy the globe."

"It almost worked," Tristan said under his breath.

Natasha gave him a curious look but did not ask what he meant. "We called off classes that week. We decided to reveal the truth to the other students, most of whom were not surprised. Then we spent every hour supervising the Map Room, waiting for Ilana to reveal herself.

"No auras appeared for several days, and we began to wonder if Ilana had fled while we were looking the other way. Then, all at once, strings of auras began appearing in small groups and then disappearing—clearly they were boarding planes or helicopters. We couldn't believe how many there were! More than fifty, possibly even a hundred."

Tristan nodded. "And most of them are still out there," he said grimly.

Just then, five waiters appeared with their food, the aroma of rich Chinese sauces, sautéed garlic, crispy orange chicken, and spicy hot and sour soup filling the room. No one spoke as the waiters set the platters and bowls down.

Once they had left, Natasha reached for a plate and spooned a large helping of moo shu vegetables onto her plate.

Impatient for her to continue, Tristan said, "But you lost us after that, didn't you? You didn't see where we went."

"There was a ship we followed for a while," Natasha said, handing the platter on to Drakewell, who grimaced. "We could only see four auras on the ship, but they were so bright we knew they were magicians. Drakewell wanted to attack it, but none of us knew if either of you were aboard.

Unfortunately, the ship disappeared into the southern hemisphere before long, and though we tried to fix the globe so we could follow them south, it was such a slow process that the ship had long since disappeared by the time we could track its course. And we can't see four stray auras on the full globe, so we had no hope of picking the ship out of the sea."

"That was our fault," Tristan said. "Ilana still didn't trust us, so we told her that the safest place to hide was somewhere in the southern hemisphere. We've been in New Zealand for the past two months."

"Oh!" Leila said. "I thought you were in Africa. That's where the ship looked like it was heading."

"They considered it," Tristan said, "but one of the teachers was a New Zealander, and he said it would be easier to go somewhere familiar."

"Well, it's a good thing you showed up before we fixed the entire globe," Quinsley said drily. "We were planning to start with Africa before moving on to South America and Australia. We probably would've fixed Antarctica before we got around to New Zealand."

Tristan laughed dully. "What happened then? What about the earthquake?"

Natasha picked up the story once more. "All this time, someone was sending drenching rain at the Lair. We knew it was Ilana, but our air magic was running so low we couldn't waste it on sending the rainclouds away."

Tristan glanced at Amber, who had ducked her head to her plate and was suddenly very interested in her sesame chicken. She would feel guilty, of course—if she had agreed to gather more air magic for the Lair, this would never have happened.

"By the time the rain had shattered our outer barrier once more, we knew Ilana had something terrible in store for us. Barely a day after the barrier came down, a catastrophic earthquake hit the valley. Most of the Lair collapsed, and those of us who were lucky enough to be near the top were able to dig our way out. As you know, we were unable to return for Delair." Natasha took a heavy breath. "That nearby cave collapsed entirely, and several large sections of rock were dislodged from the mountains.

"Luckily our plane escaped undamaged, and we flew to Millersville to recoup. We had no supplies, and aside from an account we set up with the Millersville bank, most of our wealth is still buried in the Lair. That was ten days ago. As soon as we received your message, we gathered our possessions and left Millersville behind."

Tristan and Amber looked at each other in disbelief. Somehow Tristan had imagined that life had continued as usual while they had been away; to think that the Lair was no longer waiting for them, safe and stocked with supplies and sealed off from attack...

"Where are we going now?" he asked, pushing a clump of sautéed cabbage back and forth with his fork.

"We have no idea," Alldusk said. "Millersville isn't safe, because Ilana's people know exactly where to find us. Still, we don't want to go too far from the Lair. If someone managed to raid the tunnels, we would be destroyed."

"But what happened to you?" Leila asked. "Your story is going to be so much more exciting than ours!"

"First, everyone needs to eat," Natasha said sternly. "This hot and sour soup is delicious. Would you like some, Rowan?"

Drakewell took the bowl of soup with a frown, and for a few minutes everyone fell quiet as they dug into the feast. When Tristan could eat no more, he pushed his plate away and waited for someone to ask for his side of the story again. Rajesh was eating steadily, eyes fixed on his plate, while Mei Ling picked at one piece of rice at a time with her chopsticks. Both were avoiding the curious stares of the students from the Lair. To his right, Amber's eyes had glazed over. Tristan shifted ever so slightly closer to her and pressed his knee against hers; Amber turned with a start and stared at him. After a moment, her expression of alarm softened to a shy smile.

"C'mon," Rusty said once he had polished his plate clean. "Tell us what happened!"

So Tristan began slowly, describing everything that had happened since the day he and Amber had left the Lair. He told them about being picked up almost immediately from Millersville, and about the division they had been assigned into. When he mentioned Ilana's obsession with using internal strength to fuel spells, Drakewell asked for a demonstration.

"I'm no good at it," Tristan said. "Rajesh, do you want to—?"

Though Rajesh made a face, he complied. With a

subtle gesture, all twelve candles on the table began burning so fiercely that their wax melted into one giant turquoise puddle.

"Impressive," Alldusk said, leaning back in his chair and folding his arms over his chest as the candles flickered out one by one.

"And does everyone at this school of yours possess the same talent?" Drakewell asked sharply.

Rajesh shook his head. "Only the kids in the top two divisions, and there weren't many of us. I think a couple of them might be gone now. The other divisions were learning, but most of them weren't very good at it. It takes years of strength training and concentration before you can do that."

"We are well aware of that," Drakewell said coldly. "Continue, Fairholm."

Tristan shot Rajesh an apologetic look and continued. He didn't go into detail about the punishment Ilana had put them through, and he didn't mention Merridy, though he did explain how Amber had been locked away and forced to produce a hundred air marbles before they left the ice cave behind.

"We didn't see Ilana for almost two months after that," he said. "She and a couple other teachers took the globe on a ship, and she must've sent all of that rain and the earthquake while she was on her way to New Zealand."

He described their time in the Bulmer cave system, and mentioned the way they'd been harvesting earth magic through the stalactites.

"Poor Osric would have been so excited to hear that," Gracewright said sadly.

Tristan swallowed. He was just grateful that none of his friends had been trapped down in the Subroom during the earthquake.

Leila urged him to continue, so he explained their plan to trap Ilana and the globe outside while they found a way to destroy it.

"And you actually did it?" Leila asked, wide-eyed.

"Yeah. We dropped a burning backpack full of marbles and fuel canisters over the globe, and everything for thirty feet was completely obliterated. Ilana is dead, I'm almost positive, and the teacher responsible for the First Division is too."

"How many are left?" Natasha asked.

"I don't know," Tristan said. "Four of them chased after us, and at least one of those four survived. There were probably twenty or thirty others left outside the cave when we escaped, but I don't know how many were students and how many were trained magicians. There were lots of really young kids, too, and they wouldn't know anything about magic. Ilana liked to adopt them from birth so they'd be completely brainwashed."

Drakewell's mouth twisted, but he said nothing.

"Now tell us about this spell of Ilana's," Natasha said in a low voice.

Every eye was on Tristan now. "Before we left the ice cave, Ilana told Amber that she'd found an old spell that would be more powerful than both globes combined.

That's what she needed the air magic for, and I think she must have enacted that while she was on the ship. She didn't even care about the globe by the end."

"She might have just been making that up to scare you," Quinsley said.

"No." It was the first time Amber had spoken all evening, and every head turned to her. "I can feel it. Something has taken hold up in the north. I can sense it on the wind. It grows stronger every day."

Though it was a warm evening, Tristan shivered. This was something new, something no one understood. Ilana might have known she was going to die. This ancient piece of magic must have been her way of ensuring the rest of the world would end with her.

"Can you tell us where the magic is based?" Natasha asked.

"No," Amber said softly. "I would have to search for it. But I think it lies almost directly to the north."

Tristan found her hand under the table and gave it a squeeze, trying not to imagine what waited for them.

It was a quiet group that returned to the Vancouver Bay Hotel that night. As the others began making their way up to their rooms, Tristan stopped Alldusk. "Can I talk to you?"

"Of course," Alldusk said, looking surprised.

Tristan did not want to be the one to say this, but someone had to. "Merridy was there," he said quietly. "At Ilana's school. They'd captured her and locked her up."

A spark of hope lit Alldusk's eyes, so Tristan plowed

on before his professor came to the wrong conclusion.

"We talked to her. She said she'd been wrong, said she wished she'd never left the Lair."

"Where is she now?" Alldusk asked desperately. "Is she—"

Tristan shook his head. "Ilana killed her." His voice broke. "I'm so sorry."

Alldusk froze. His face went grey, and his hands shook slightly. But when he spoke, his voice was surprisingly steady. "Thank you for telling me. It is a small reassurance to know that she forgave us in the end."

"I'm so sorry," Tristan repeated uselessly.

"It's okay," Alldusk said, running a trembling hand through his black hair. "Get some rest. And don't worry about me."

Tristan hesitated before continuing down the hall. When he looked over his shoulder as he waited for the elevator, Alldusk was gone.

Rusty was waiting for him on the tenth floor. "Where'd you disappear off to?"

"I just had to talk to Alldusk," Tristan said, shoving his hands into his pockets. "Merridy was locked up at Ilana's school, but she's dead now."

Rusty rocked back on his heels. "Poor Alldusk!"

"I know." He had looked forward to this reunion for months, but now the evening had turned bitter, tainted by death and by the thought of what might have happened to Pavlina and Ori.

When Tristan made to turn into the room he'd been

sharing with Amber, Rajesh, and Mei Ling, Rusty grabbed his arm and steered him across the hall. "Everyone's here. They wanna spend some time with you."

"Where are Rajesh and Mei Ling?"

Rusty glanced back at the door across the hall. "They're probably in there."

Tristan shook his arm free and went to fetch his new friends. "I'd be dead without them," he told Rusty over his shoulder. "I don't want them to regret coming with us." He opened the door and called, "Rajesh? Mei Ling? You have to come meet the others properly."

Mei Ling appeared at once, toothbrush in her mouth. "Okay!"

Rajesh poked his head around the corner a moment later. "Do we have to? I'm tired."

"Oh, come on," Tristan said. "If you're going to stay with us, you'll have to get to know everyone a bit better."

Several minutes later, they joined him in the hallway, Mei Ling looking excited, Rajesh scowling.

"This is Rusty," Tristan said, tilting his head at his friend.

Grinning, Rusty shook both of their hands. "It's exciting, getting new kids here," he said. "There's only fifteen of us—well, thirteen once Tristan and Amber were gone—and it gets kinda boring after a while."

"Only fifteen?" Rajesh said skeptically. "Ilana was so worried about your school. I don't think she realized how small it was."

"We also had the Lair," Tristan said. "That's much

safer than Ilana's ice cave. Or it was, anyway. Come on. Let's get this over with." He was tired himself, and already overwhelmed after seeing everyone again for the first time in months.

When Rusty led the way into the bedroom across the hall, the four of them were greeted with applause.

"Oh, calm down," Tristan said, trying not to smile. "It hasn't been *that* long."

"Look what Gerry slipped us," Leila said, holding up a bottle of champagne.

They had secured a spacious suite with a sitting area and three plush couches, and Tristan's friends were sitting all around the room, some perched on the end of the single enormous bed, others curled up with their backs against the wall. Amber was there, to his relief, and she gave him a shy smile from her seat in the back corner.

As Tristan took a seat beside Leila on one of the couches, Rajesh and Mei Ling settling awkwardly onto the end of the bed behind him, he did a double-take. Was that *Zeke* sitting next to Trey?

"What's up with you?" Tristan asked Zeke, though without malice.

Zeke gave him a funny smile. "Damian and Cassidy haven't talked to me in weeks. And these morons are stupid enough to hang out with me in the meantime."

Tristan raised his eyebrows at Leila, who punched him in the shoulder. "Oh, shut up," she muttered.

"What else is new?" Tristan asked, taking a wine glass from Hayley. She continued around the room, passing out a mismatched collection of water glasses, mugs, and wine glasses that had clearly been scavenged from several different rooms.

"We didn't get to go home for summer," Rusty said. "It's too dangerous now. But I got to visit Christa a month ago." His tone softened. "She's out of Juvie now, and she's staying with a really nice foster family. Alldusk helped arrange the whole thing."

Leila pried off the wire cage over the champagne cork, tongue between her teeth.

"What about classes?" Tristan asked. "You haven't just been carrying on like usual, have you?"

"Like Natasha said, we stayed in normal classes for the first month or two," Cailyn said. "After that, we started watching the Map Room with them and learning as much defensive magic as possible. We spent a lot of time up in the forest, which was nice. No one was watching us any longer, and I think Natasha knew we might be evacuating the Lair before long. We spent a week hiking through the woods with Gracewright at one point, and we learned how to forage and make shelters from everything we could find."

When the champagne was poured, they all raised their glasses.

"To Tristan and Amber," Leila said.

"Tristan and Amber," repeated everyone except Tristan and Amber.

The bubbles tickled his throat as he took a sip, leaning back into the embroidered couch pillows. "Damian's gang is going to be looking pretty sad," he remarked, allowing the weight of fear and sorrow to retreat just for a short while.

Eli laughed. "I don't see them joining us, though. They'll just be wallowing in their misery, champagne-less and lonely."

They spent the next several hours in happy companionship, joking and catching up on all the mundane details of life the others had missed. Even Rajesh and Mei Ling joined the circle after a while, though Rajesh still looked uncomfortable.

It was well past midnight when Tristan, Amber, Rajesh, and Mei Ling returned to their room. After the clean room they had just left, the stench of camping gear and mildew was stronger than ever.

As Tristan pushed open the door, he caught sight of a postcard in the shape of a maple leaf lying on the floor. What was that doing back here?

He bent to pick it up. The spiked handwriting was unfamiliar, but his heartbeat quickened as he began to read.

We'll be waiting for you. You're not half as clever as you think you are.

Tristan handed the postcard wordlessly to Rajesh.

"Mordechai," Rajesh whispered.

Mei Ling's eyes widened. "Even here?"

"It's not over yet," Tristan said. He locked deadbolt and crossed to his bed, the words still seared across his eyes. *We'll be waiting for you.* But where? Was Mordechai in Millersville, or had he broken into the Lair?

The curtains rippled in a warm breeze, and beyond them, the night was waiting.

The end

Acknowledgments

That this series has made it thus far is due in large part to my wonderful readers.

Special thanks goes to my launch team, who have been there at the times it mattered most.

Also to my editors—this book came together under the expert guidance of Melinda, Kayla, Nancy, and Bill.

To the wonderful 10k Angels, for encouraging me when my motivation was flagging…

And most of all, to my husband Daniel, who gave me the opportunity to write full-time for the first three months of this year, during which time this book came to life. None of this would have been possible without his support.

About the Author

R.J. Vickers is the author of the Natural Order series, as well as *Beauty's Songbook*, a Beauty and the Beast retelling, and *College Can Wait!*, a gap year guidebook for reluctant students.

When she's not writing, you can find her hiking, traveling, taking photos, and crocheting.

Though she grew up in Colorado, she now lives with her husband in New Zealand.

You can find her online at rjvickers.com.

CPSIA information can be obtained
at www.ICGtesting.com
Printed in the USA
FSHW01n0728200518
48472FS